"Dad," Delia began, "do you suppose you can do me a favor?"

"And what might that be?"

"Next time you're shopping for music, would you buy me some Chopin? The pianist plays a lot of Chopin in ballet class." Delia hesitated to say more. It felt like she was telling a wish after blowing out the candles on a birthday cake.

"What a lovely request! I'm so pleased you like your new teacher. If only your sister hadn't stopped dancing. Pearl is so expressive in her way. . . . Perhaps, ah, but how can a parent ever really know . . ." He looked sadly into the distance.

Delia was accustomed to the way her father spoke about Pearl in unfinished sentences. Maybe he stopped himself because he didn't want Delia to know all the details of Pearl's problems. *This is silly*, she thought. She knew more than he thought she did.

TRACEY PORTER

A Dance of Sisters

JOANNA COTLER BOOKS

HarperTrophy®

An Imprint of HarperCollins*Publishers*

Quote on page 266 reprinted from *The Ghost Dance*, by James Mooney, page 432, copyright 1996. Reprinted by permission of World Publications Group Inc.

A Dance of Sisters

Library of Congress Cataloging-in-Publication Data
Porter, Tracey.
A dance of sisters / by Tracey Porter.
    p.   cm.
Summary: Although almost totally consumed by her ballet training and her obsession with controlling her weight, thirteen-year-old Delia finds time to worry about her strange and rebellious older sister Pearl, who has been sent away to a private school.
    ISBN 0-06-028182-0 — 0-06-440751-9 (pbk.)
    [1. Ballet dancing—Fiction. 2. Sisters—Fiction. 3. Anorexia nervosa—Fiction.] I. Title.
PZ7.P83395 Dan 2002   2001051544
[Fic]—dc21   CIP
                                                                   AC

Typography by Alicia Mikles
❖
First Harper Trophy edition, 2005
Visit us on the World Wide Web!
www.harperchildrens.com

ACKNOWLEDGMENTS

I would like to thank the following people for helping me with this book:

Justin Chanda and Joanna Cotler for their faith and guidance.

My brother, James, for his loving support.

Jeannie Jacobson for sharing her insights and her beautiful dancing.

Linda Yudin for our talks about orishas.

Doug Thompson for his help with Portuguese.

My inspiring girlfriends: Michelle Mansfield, Gabriel Firth, Liz Lane, Lori Michelle Newsom, Sasha Emerson, Sarah Torgov, Annetta Kapon, Kristi Henry, Carole Winter, and Francesca Lia Block.

The students in my red core class for their interest and opinions.

My wonderful parents, and my loving husband, Sandy, for being there in a thousand different ways.

I would especially like to thank my mother, Susan, who gave me all the ballet classes I wanted, and my dear friend Karuna who helped me survive them.

For my daughter, Sarah

1

Sisters

It was Pearl who gave Delia her nickname Little Moon, and it was Pearl who taught Delia about loss, magic, and change. But even though they loved each other, they circled like planets, one catching light, the other lapsing into darkness, often in view but always distant.

It was spring in Washington, D.C. Thick maples arched overhead. Delia was six. Pearl was ten, dressed as Persephone for her class play about the Greek gods. They held hands as they walked home from school.

"Artemis is the goddess of the moon, and sometimes the Greeks called her Delia. So, I will call you Little Moon, because you are named after Artemis and you are my little sister."

Delia dropped her head with pride, watching her feet on the familiar sidewalk home, each crack and leaf imprint both friendly and strange.

Neighbors watered new lawns, and the two left brief, dark footsteps.

"Little Moon," Delia whispered to herself, learning the rise and fall of consonants, the feel of the words in her mouth.

The air was drenched with sun. It fell from the sky, bounced off the chrome of the cars, and filled forsythia bushes in their front yard with light. Pearl's white costume and blond hair absorbed the glow of the yellow flowers, and for the moment before she opened the front door, she looked like she was spun from gold.

Delia often remembered that day, how their footprints dried so quickly, and how her sister transformed before her eyes. She used to pretend Pearl was her mother. She could not remember her real mother. She died before Delia could talk.

Now it was more than seven years later, a bleak September afternoon, and Delia and Pearl were again a doorway apart. Where was Pearl now, Delia wondered as she waited for her sister to open her door.

"Yes?" Pearl left the chain on the door and opened it a crack. Her face was powdered geisha white and her eyes were lined with black. A sweet scent wafted into the hall. Delia sniffed. Baby oil. Pearl had just worked some into her hair. The comb's teeth cut neat, greasy rows close to the scalp so that it looked like the plastic molded hair of a doll.

"Do you have the sewing box?" Delia asked. "I need to sew elastic on my new shoes before class." She held a new pair of ballet slippers in her left hand.

"Come in," Pearl sang. She unlocked the

door and beckoned her in with a little bow. "Sit down." She motioned to the hot-pink beanbag chair and turned down the music.

"Thanks," Delia replied, surprised that her sister had allowed her the privilege of entering. She flopped in the chair and briskly scanned the room while her sister's back was turned. She hadn't been here in a long time. Vases of rotting marigolds in murky water, framed photographs of dead poets and musicians, sugar skulls with tin eyes, candles and incense burners covered the desk. A black Spanish shawl embroidered with red and pink roses hung over the window and blocked the sun. A line of blue sand circled the canopy bed, the same pink frilly one Pearl had slept in since she was three. *Great*, thought Delia, *she's casting spells again*.

"I like the shawl," Delia said. It was best not to bring up the sand. Pearl might get angry at her for snooping and throw her out before giving her a needle and thread. Or, she might go into elaborate detail about her latest spell and make her late for ballet.

"Thanks. Twelve dollars at a junk store on Fourteenth Street." Pearl opened the closet door and began picking through a tangled pile of black clothes.

"And when were you on Fourteenth Street?" Their father encouraged them to be city children, to take the subway to the museums, or to walk to Georgetown. But that part of the city was forbidden to them, and as far as Delia was concerned, there was no reason to go there.

"Don't worry, Little Moon. Summer and Locke were with me."

"I'm sure they felt right at home," Delia retorted. She pictured Pearl and her two friends roaming the junk shops and botanicas between the various bars and liquor stores. Summer with her bedraggled black boa around her neck, Locke in his mohawk, Pearl in the dress with the vampire sleeves. "You shouldn't go there. Dad would kill you if he found out."

"Well, don't tell him, Little Moon . . ." She tossed a black tulle petticoat over her back. It landed in Delia's lap. "Besides, I gotta go. The best botanica in town is there— Espiritu del Mundo. Madame Congo is ordering a bunch of stuff for me."

"I hope you're not getting any more of those dried lizards. They totally grossed me out." Pearl had taken her to a botanica once. Black, red, and white candles shaped like humans, wands of incense, statues of saints filled the shelves. Along the walls were huge barrels, just like in a candy shop, only these were filled with strange-smelling powders, colored sand, and dried herbs. She shuddered when she saw the packages of tiny bones.

"I'm not into that stuff anymore. I'm into healing, not cursing."

"That's a relief," said Delia. She played with her hair while she waited. She braided it and shook it free. It was thick and dark like their mother's, the only trait of hers that she had. Pearl, their father once said, was her mirror image.

"Eureka!" Pearl exclaimed moments later. She handed Delia the wicker sewing basket, stuffed the clothes and shoes back into the closet, then flopped on her canopy bed.

It was the same basket their mother had used. Inside were buttons made of shell and bone, wooden spools of colored thread, and packages of needles and snaps. When they were little, Pearl taught her how to cut out paper dolls with the gold scissors shaped like a stork. *Babies,* Delia thought, remembering the image of baby and stork as she cut the pink elastic in half. *My sister and I were babies once.* It was hard to imagine. It seemed that her father needed her to grow up quickly, and she did her best to comply. As for Pearl, well, she had always seemed grown-up.

Pearl lounged on her bed, watching her sister sew elastic to the inside of her slippers. She yawned, and her white skin peeked through dozens of little slits she had cut into the bodice of her old black dress.

"Why don't you keep the pink thread in your room," she said. "I never use it. Take a couple of needles, too."

"Thanks," said Delia. It was an unusual show of generosity. Pearl hoarded the sewing supplies. She loved tearing clothes apart and turning them into her own design. She traded collars and sleeves, skirts and bodices. The styles changed constantly, but ever since the fire, the only color she wore was black.

A year ago, while their father was out, Pearl had pulled stones from the crumbling wall in the alley, transported them in the old red wagon and arranged them in a circle in their backyard.

"What are you doing?" she asked when Pearl came stomping upstairs. Pearl said nothing. She squeezed past Delia and slammed the door to her room. A few moments later she emerged with a mountain of clothes in her arms. Her red and white cheerleader skirt fell to the floor. Delia picked it up and followed her outside.

"You dropped this," she offered, searching her sister's face for a clue. She found none. Pearl snatched the skirt out of her hands.

"I need a little space right now," she said. "Why don't you go watch TV."

"Can I help?"

"No. Go watch TV."

Instead Delia sneaked upstairs to watch from the window in the hall.

Pearl stripped naked, stepped next to the circle, and spoke aloud. She tossed her clothes into the circle, doused them with lighter fluid, and set them on fire. She stoked the fire with a stick. Sparks ascended to the sky and died. Ashy bits of burned cloth floated in the air like moths.

Delia peered out the window. Bare branches of the maple tree rattled in the wind. She wondered if she should call her father at the number he had left, or if she should wait up to tell him when he got home. "You won't believe what Pearl did . . ." she imagined telling him. In the end she did nothing. He would find out soon enough.

Since then Pearl had pulled further and further away from the two of them. She put a lock on her door, painted her face with white makeup, and wore black. She rarely spoke of school or friends or much of anything at home. Every now and then, in a sudden burst of affection, she showered Delia with attention. She would sew her a new dance bag or take her to a movie. But mostly she kept to herself, and Delia often felt lonesome in her own house.

"Is Dad driving you to class, or are you taking the bus?" Pearl asked.

"I'm taking the bus." Delia finished sewing the last elastic into place. She broke the thread with her teeth and twisted the ends into a tiny knot.

"Do you want me to drive you?"

"I thought you were on restriction," Delia answered.

"Restriction? What did I do this time?"

"You skipped school," Delia answered, trying to control the anger in her voice. The least Pearl could do was remember what she did wrong. She made their father worry constantly, and she didn't even care.

"Oh, right," Pearl mused. "Summer wanted to see the baby gorilla at the zoo."

"I don't know why you didn't wait for the weekend. You're at a small private school. Of course you're going to get caught if you skip."

"Not necessarily," said Pearl professionally. "Country Day is just like any other private school, hoping to make a difference in the lives of troubled teens so their parents will make a big donation. They ignore when I break the rules until they absolutely have to take a stand. Private schools are all the same."

You should know, thought Delia. Pearl had

been expelled from three. If she didn't succeed at Columbia Country Day, her father threatened to send her to a girls' boarding school in Pennsylvania.

"I better go," said Delia. "Thanks for letting me do my sewing in your room."

"Anytime," answered Pearl. "Well, not anytime, but, you know . . . Every now and then is nice. Have a good class."

Outside the day was losing light. Dry leaves sounded like paper in the wind. With each step away from her house, Delia felt more airy and distant. Thoughts about Pearl, worries that she might get expelled or run away, began to fade. She was glad. *Maybe I'll finally have a good class.*

Delia sat at the bench waiting for the bus to take her down Wisconsin Avenue to the Elanova School of Ballet. She slipped her hand into her ballet bag to touch her new shoes. She had been studying at the Elanova School for only a few months, and she did not have any friends yet. That was all right with her. She appreciated the chance to be silent. There was no one to say hello to, no one to chat with. She thought of the opportunities to work on the line of her leg in developpés at the barre and in the adagio in the center. *I want to stretch to the moon*, Delia thought. *Far, far away.*

2

Sylphs

The lobby of the Elanova School smelled like stale perfume and old wool. It reminded Delia of the Italian train stations she saw when her father took his daughters with him to buy ovens for his new bakeries. Small groups of people waited together, and a sense of purpose and expectation filled the room. A statue of Mary looked down from a tiny altar in a corner of the lobby. Here, at the Elanova School, the sense of purpose was for the dance, and the overriding presence, the being looking down from on high, was Madame Alicia Elanova.

Even the youngest girls playing cards outside

Studio I spoke softly. Mothers sat on the threadbare sofa, gossiping and knitting. The older girls dominated the hall with their stretching, splitting their legs against the wall, lying prone, legs bent in frog position to loosen their hip joints. Others waited in the dressing room, pinning their leotards so their bra straps wouldn't show or banging new pointe shoes against the tiled shower to soften their sound on the studio's wooden floor. In the far corner near the showers two anorexic girls whispered together between sips of coffee. They dressed identically in gray rubber sweat pants and pale pink long-sleeved leotards.

Across from the entrance was the office where the tireless Miss Dairy, Madame's assistant, served as bookkeeper, receptionist, nurse, and fountain of information. She was nearsighted and expressionless, always at odds with the mountain of paperwork stacked on her desk. Farther down the hall, another door led to Madame's apartment, which consisted of the entire third floor of the building. Between these two doors, a tarnished samovar rested on a rosewood table. Above was a large portrait of Madame Elanova, a photograph taken shortly after she was named ballerina with Les Ballets Russes. She was only seventeen, but already she donned a regal, aloof expression. Her shoulders were bare. Around her neck she wore the ruby necklace a member of the Russian royal family had given her after seeing her dance the role of Giselle. Delia always glanced at the portrait on her way to the dressing room.

Four months ago, Delia had left Miss Sherrie's World of Dance, where she had been taking class since she was six. Miss Sherrie was mostly concerned with training well-rounded dancers who could perform in her yearly recitals. She considered ballroom, tap, and jazz as important as ballet, and she was surprised when Delia said she wanted to take only ballet and dropped out of the spring recital. She had cast her in the jazz number, a dance for twelve girls called "Jazz Kittens."

"I need a strong dancer like you to help the others remember the steps. You're going to be in the front row. Look at your costume." She held out a catalogue of recital costumes and pointed to a girl in a hot-pink cheetah print unitard with little triangle ears and a long, swishy black tail.

Delia looked politely at the picture, but remained steadfast. *There has to be more to dance than this*, Delia thought. She felt it in the scratchy records Miss Sherrie played for class. Music drifted in from another class and told her she was right.

"I'm sorry, Miss Sherrie. I just can't this year. I have so much schoolwork . . ." And so, when it was time to sign up for another series of classes at Miss Sherrie's school, Delia told her father not to write the check.

She had seen the Elanova School of Ballet

many times as she walked to Georgetown to browse in the stores or see a film. It rose above the street on a small hill, a dilapidated white mansion choked with wisteria, nearly hidden by elms. It seemed to be a dreary, run-down studio with its faded sign and worn stairway. Pale, serious girls took lessons there. Delia saw them waiting at the bus stop or hailing a taxi.

One Sunday shortly after her disenchantment with Miss Sherrie, Delia was leafing through *Dance Magazine* while her father bought the new cycling magazine at their local newsstand. She became engrossed in a lengthy article entitled "The Ten Best Ballet Teachers Outside of New York." A photograph of a girl in first arabesque on pointe caught her eye. Her strong legs tapered to delicately arched feet, and she lightly held the hand of her teacher, an older woman whose face she couldn't see. "Madame Alicia Elanova," the caption read, "has been providing the purest Russian training in the country for over twenty years."

The article went on to list some of the professional dancers who had trained with her, and even though Delia had not heard of many of them, their names were lyrical and alluring, the names of dancers. They danced in companies in New York and Europe, and all of them said Madame was their greatest teacher. Delia thought of all the great Russian dancers she knew—Pavlova, Nijinsky, Makarova, and Baryshnikov—and she knew she wanted that world with its discipline and beauty.

"I want to study with her," Delia said, pointing to the photo in the magazine. "Her studio is just down the street from us."

Her father studied the picture briefly. "Oh, yes! Her school is in that old house on Wisconsin. It's close. You can take the bus. Find out how much it costs, and I'll write the check."

And so in September she began her studies at the Elanova School.

The girls in Delia's intermediate class

brushed past her in the changing room, giggling among themselves, as if she did not exist. Delia put her overalls and shoes in a locker and snapped the padlock shut.

Slowly but surely, she was learning the Elanova School's unspoken rules of manners and decorum by watching the better dancers in the advanced class. One could glimpse them as they lingered in the studio after class, practicing pirouettes or shuffling back to the dressing room, pointe shoes off to air their blistered feet, back curved with the weight of an overstuffed ballet bag. Only the strongest dancers adorned themselves with plain black or pink chiffon skirts. Delia wondered how these girls knew they were allowed to wear leg warmers and skirts. Did Madame tell them, or did they figure it out all on their own?

In the studio, the girls in Delia's class chatted and stretched aimlessly at the barre. Mr. Guest, the ancient pianist, stared blankly into space, sipping tea. Miss Tupine had not arrived. Delia thought she was a good teacher, even if she did ignore the stragglers who couldn't remember the combination. She did not help anyone whom she felt wasn't trying her best. Delia watched and listened carefully.

Suddenly, there was a collective intake of breath. Girls halted their chatting and removed legs from the barre. Delia turned to see Madame Elanova herself sweep into the studio. She had never seen her in real life, but she recognized her from the portrait and her faded photos in the hall. She embodied the authority of a queen and was dressed in a long flowing skirt, leotard top, and a pastel print scarf about the throat. She smiled gaily at the crumpled Mr. Guest, and, by her mere presence alone, commanded the girls to a dignified attention. Automatically, all twenty-five of them stepped into first position at the barre and awaited her instruction. Even Mr. Guest took note. He put down his tea and sat taller in his chair. Impressed by the air of serious-ness in the room, Delia imitated what she saw.

"Good afternoon," she announced to the class. "Miss Tupine, alas, is sick. I vill teach class today. Is good for me, no? For I see for myself who is ready to join me in Pointes Three. Mr. Guest, today I vant nice Chopin nocturne for pliés. You know my favorite . . ."

Then, with more expressiveness than Delia had ever heard in his playing before, Mr. Guest began the Nocturne in B-flat Major, op. 9, no. 3. Class had begun.

Elegant and easy to remember, Madame's combinations were more difficult than they seemed. There were no brain-teasing reversals of steps. Instead, phrases of movement were lyrical and fluid. Long full counts were given to things as simple as a port de bras. "Feel the music!" she commanded as she luxuriated in demonstrating exactly what she wanted to see. She glanced approvingly at a few girls, watched others out of the corner of her eye, and whispered to herself in Russian throughout the class.

In the middle of the allegro combination, she suddenly became angry.

"Stop the music!" Madame shouted at Mr. Guest. The melody fell into shards of broken notes. "You! Leetle girl vith black ribbon in hair. Remove your gum." Madame pointed to a small wastepaper basket near the door. Delia could see the back of the girl's ears turn pink as she walked to the front of the studio. Delia felt afraid for her.

"Now, go to office and call your mother. Tell her to pick you up early. There is no more ballet for you today." The girl wilted with distress. Mr. Guest coughed loudly. The girl picked up her things and left.

Delia shuddered slightly. Nothing like this had ever happened at Miss Sherrie's World of Dance. To be reprimanded and told to leave in front of the class, surely nothing could be worse. She prayed silently for a moment that nothing like that would ever happen to her.

The girl's dismissal was strangely motivating. Delia felt herself and the class work harder. No one wanted to displease Madame again. Extensions were higher, balances longer. Girls left the floor after completing a combination as if they were exiting into the wings of an opera house. Delia left with her arms in first arabesque, her gaze skimming the line of her arm and peering into the distance.

As far as Delia could tell, Madame had absolutely no interest in her. She gave her no corrections, no smiles, no words of criticism, praise, or encouragement. Delia was sure Madame felt she was too weak a student to be bothered with.

Class ended in the traditional way at the Elanova School, one of the many traditions Madame modeled on her own training at the Imperial Ballet School in Russia. One by one, students placed their right hand in both of

Madame's, curtseyed, and said, "Thank you, Madame."

Delia hung at the back of the studio, rummaging through her ballet bag, not sure if she should do as the others or not. After all, she was new at the school. She and Madame had never met before. But before Delia could slip out the back door of the studio, Madame caught her with an inviting expression. As if she had been silently commanded, which indeed she had been, Delia walked up to Madame, extended her hand, curtseyed, and whispered a thank you. Madame Elanova did not release her. Instead, she pulled Delia slightly closer, looked in her eyes, and said, "Beautiful girl, do you know how God has blessed you vith those feet? Those legs? Point your foot for me. Let me feast on your beauty once more." Delia stood there sheepishly in pointe tendu écarté as Madame inspected the arch of her foot. "Ahhh! Like Pavlova's, your feet. Girls, girls!" She called to the girls hovering about the piano, the same girls who had ignored her for weeks. "Do you know vhat a sylph you have in your class? Vhat is your name, darling? Do you know the new girl, Celia Ferri? How beautiful she is!"

Delia barely noticed that Madame had confused her name. She was overwhelmed with a mixture of pride and embarrassment. She responded with a shy smile and pulled away, keeping her eyes to the floor as she rushed off to the dressing room. She felt the girls at the piano staring as she left.

Delia's father was waiting in the car in the parking lot reading a cycling magazine. He didn't know Delia was there until she opened the door. He looked up briefly.

"Just let me finish this page," he said. He read another moment then tossed the magazine in the backseat.

"Do you know why the Italians are the greatest cyclists? It's because they begin their serious training when they're your age. Your age!"

"I believe it," said Delia, perturbed that her father didn't realize his own daughter was in serious training herself. *But it's not his fault*, she reminded herself. *He worries about Pearl so much.*

"Do you know what I was doing when I was your age? Working in the bakery, carrying fifty-pound sacks of flour, sweeping the floor, getting up before dawn to help my dad bake the first dozen loaves of bread . . ."

It was already dark as night, and a few shy stars began to tremble and blink.

"How was class?" her father finally asked.

"Fine," Delia answered. She tucked in a loose hairpin and wondered what else to say. How could she explain what had happened in class? For a moment she wondered if she was living the recurring dream she had about her home. Suddenly a door appears where before there was only a bare wall. A long hallway spills into a vast, blue room, and Delia sees that it is open to the sky.

"It was better than fine," Delia offered. "Miss Tupine was sick so Madame Elanova taught. It was a pretty class."

"Great! That's what I like to hear in my daughter—enthusiasm. I wish your sister could get some enthusiasm about something."

"She's enthusiastic about witchcraft and black clothes," Delia replied.

"Don't remind me."

Delia sighed. When Pearl criticized her father, Delia felt compelled to speak up for him. And, when her father criticized Pearl, she felt compelled to speak up for her.

"At least she's her own person. She doesn't want to be anyone but herself," said Delia. She wished her father could appreciate at least this about her.

"I wouldn't mind if Pearl were more of a conformer. It would bring me some relief."

Mr. Ferri turned on the radio. They didn't

speak for the rest of the way home. Delia turned her face to the side window. She watched the trees appear and disappear in the lights of passing cars, remembering how it felt to be told she was beautiful.

3

Sugar

As usual, Pearl was running late. Delia had finished her cereal by the time Pearl stumbled bleary-eyed into the breakfast room. Shunning the croissants her father brought home from the bakery, she crumbled two powdered doughnuts into a bowl. She sprinkled them with a heaping spoonful of sugar, poured a glass of milk over the whole thing, and began to eat. Three drops of sugary milk fell just below the collar of her black dress.

"I have a test first period. Can you believe it?"

"What on?" Delia asked.

Pearl considered the question carefully, playing with her spoon as if she were writing a sentence in the air. "I'm not sure," she answered.

A horn honked three times. It was the Columbia Country Day minibus and Pearl should have been waiting outside. Delia could tell the driver was angry from the rhythm of the beeps.

"Damn! Be a gumdrop, Little Moon, and go get my backpack. I've got to secure my sugar rush."

"Why should I?" asked Delia. She turned away from her sister to rinse out her cereal bowl and put it in the dishwasher.

"Because I let you use the needle and thread yesterday. Please do it for me. Pretty please. It's upstairs under the table in the hall." The driver honked again.

Delia groaned from the tension she felt. She looked at Pearl drinking the last milky crumbs from her bowl as if it were a cup, and she heard the driver pounding the horn as if he might explode with irritation. She stomped upstairs and got the backpack.

"That driver's gonna be so mad at you," said Delia as she handed it to Pearl.

"Not to worry. I'm bringing him doughnuts, see?" She waved a plastic bag containing two doughnuts as if she were teasing a dog. Delia couldn't help but smile. Laughing, Pearl made her exit in a flurry of black.

"Did she make it?" Her father stood on the landing above the foyer, sipping the last of his cappuccino. The oversize cup hit the saucer with a porcelain clink. Delia gave her report.

"Barely. I think she's charmed the bus driver with powdered doughnuts."

"Good God," he said. As the son and grandson of bakers and the owner of three suddenly chic bakeries, Mr. Ferri was as disgusted with his daughter's choice of pastries as

with her choice of clothes. For a while he for-
bade the presence of doughnuts in his house.
But when Pearl was caught stealing a package
from a nearby convenience store, he relented.
"And what was my oldest daughter wearing
this morning?"

"Something black."

"Of course," he sighed. "Why do I even
ask?" His cycling shoes made a multitude of
taps as he marched to the kitchen to rinse his
cup. He wore the complete uniform, including
helmet, of an Italian racing team. He looked,
Pearl and Delia had decided over breakfast
one Sunday, ridiculous. Two years ago, he had
taken up cycling and had become increasingly
obsessed. He was training for a three-hundred-
mile ride that raised money for AIDS
research. After the race, he planned to add
swimming and jogging to his regimen so that
in another year he could compete in an over-
fifty triathlon. Fitness, heart rate, diet, choles-
terol, "hitting the wall, pushing past the wall,"

were all he talked about now. He rarely ate the cakes or pastries from his bakeries anymore, and he frequently lectured his daughters on the dangers of sugar, butter, and eggs.

"Dad," Delia began, "do you suppose you can do me a favor?"

"And what might that be?"

"Next time you're shopping for music, would you buy me some Chopin? I want the nocturnes."

"With pleasure! I was just thinking about buying some new CDs myself. Some Puccini, I think. And why Chopin?"

"Oh, I don't know. . . . The pianist plays a lot of Chopin in ballet class." Delia hesitated to say more. It felt like she was telling a wish after blowing out the candles on a birthday cake.

"What a lovely request! I'm so pleased you like your new teacher. If only your sister hadn't stopped dancing. Pearl is so expressive in her way. . . . Perhaps, ah, but how can a parent ever really know . . ." He looked sadly into the distance.

Delia was accustomed to the way her father spoke about Pearl in unfinished sentences. She was not sure why he did so. Maybe he was afraid that if he said his fears out loud, they would come true. Maybe he stopped himself because he didn't want Delia to know all the details of Pearl's problems. *This is silly*, she thought. She knew more than he thought she did.

Mr. Ferri dried his cup and saucer with a linen towel and returned them to the cupboard. "Wish me a good ride, Delia."

"Have a good ride, Dad." He would be gone for hours, cycling the paths of Rock Creek Parkway first, then over to Capitol Hill before coming home.

Delia made her way through the crowded halls of Markham Middle School, her backpack stuffed with books and ballet clothes. She planned to change at lunch so that she would have time for a good warm-up before her four o'clock class. A dark-haired girl walking toward her suddenly stopped.

"Hey! I know you. You're Madame's new sylph."

Delia noticed the girl's long skinny legs and the turned-out feet. Yes, she was a ballet dancer, a student in Miss Tupine's class.

"I suppose I am," said Delia. "Whatever that means . . ."

"It means plenty . . . envy from others . . . Madame always watching you even when she pretends not to . . . a good role in *Nutcracker* . . . You'll probably be moved to Pointes Three soon."

"Are you in Pointes Three?" It was the highest pointe class at the school, and only the best and most serious students took it.

"Yes. My mother received Madame's fateful call last month. 'Eees time for Pointes Three. Must vork very, very hard on pulling knees. Like scissors I vant her legs, sharp and straight like scissors!'" The girl extended her hand. "I'm Claire Acton, second generation Elanova School dancer. My mother studied with Madame for twelve years and was a dance major at Bennington."

"Hello," Delia replied, shaking her hand. "I'm Delia Ferri. Did your mother dance professionally?"

"No. She broke her ankle sophomore year and had to give up pointe. She switched to modern for a while, but she didn't like it. Mommy says ballet broke her heart. Then she met my father. He's an ornithologist at the Smithsonian."

"What's that?"

"A scientist who studies birds." She rose on pointe in her clogs and flapped her wings like the Dying Swan. Delia noticed how pretty Claire's arches looked and made a mental note to buy some clogs. A small thorn of envy pricked her. She touched her dark hair. How wonderful it must be to have a mother who danced. You could point to your turnout, the line of your leg, or the tilt of your head in attitude, and say, "This is where that comes from. I have this because of her."

"My father is a baker," said Delia. "He owns the La Traviata bakeries in Chevy Chase and Georgetown."

"How awful for you!" Claire gasped. "You must be tempted to eat pastries all the time! How do you stay so thin?"

"I'm not so thin." Delia instinctively pulled her stomach in. "I'm not that interested in pastries."

The bell rang.

"Gotta dash. See you in class." Claire rose on the pointes of her clogs, bourréed into the crowd with a laugh, and disappeared.

While her English teacher rambled on about transitive and intransitive verbs, Delia sketched pointe shoes in her notebook and wondered about her new friend. She had noticed her before because of her excellent extension and triple pirouettes. She liked how Claire dared to imitate Madame's accent. It would be nice to stretch with her before class.

The house was silent when Delia came home from school. Her father was upstairs in his office. Surprisingly, he was wearing a suit.

"Your sister didn't go to school today," he announced.

"But I saw her get on the bus."

"Well, she may have taken the bus to school, but she never made it to first period. She and Summer decided to skip school and go downtown. They were arrested for shoplifting two silver bracelets at a jewelry store."

"Is she in jail?" An image of her sister behind bars with greasy hair and a forlorn expression formed in her mind.

"No. She and Summer are being held at the police station, but if I don't get there soon they'll be transferred to the juvenile detention center. I was waiting for you to come home before I left."

"Do you think you'll be back in time to pick me up from ballet?"

"Who knows . . ." He groaned. He stuffed a twenty-dollar bill in her hand. "Take a cab home." He dropped his head in his hands. "Delia," he said, "I am so sick of Pearl's rebellion phase!"

Delia smoothed out the money and folded it into her pocket, taking time to think about what to say.

"Dad, I don't think she's rebelling. I think . . . it's something else. I think . . ." She lifted her hands, as if she were holding the mystery of Pearl's sadness to examine and dissect.

"If you figure it out, let me know. I've tried everything. I've taken her to psychiatrists, nutritionists, allergists, psychologists, homeopaths, therapists, tutors. . . . Everyone has a different theory. No one agrees. Can you name one thing that I haven't done for her? One thing I haven't given her?"

"It's not about doing something for her or giving her something. It's . . ." What did she see when she looked at her sister? The peace sign pinpricked into her arm, the black clothes, the face hidden behind the layers of makeup? Delia could not put her feelings into words.

"And her clothes!" he went on. "This is Washington, not Amsterdam or London. It's the most conservatively dressed national capital in the world. I can't stand it when she walks into my bakery in some black tattered dress with a skull necklace coiled around her neck. The head of the Ritz was there the other day placing an order for a Senate committee luncheon, and I almost hit the floor when she yelled out, 'Hi, Pop!' She's angry, and she's getting her revenge by embarrassing me."

"No, Dad. Really, I think it's something else. I think . . ." But her father wasn't listening.

It was just as well, for she did not know what else to say.

"How I hate that necklace! That necklace and that makeup are what I hate most of all. As soon as I get the lock off her door I'm going to throw them in the trash."

Delia sighed. She wandered into the kitchen to eat an apple before ballet. At the table she touched a thick, sticky drop of sugary milk from Pearl's breakfast. She tasted its sweetness, the sweetness Pearl craved. *What's wrong with Pearl?* It was as if the sister Delia used to know had fallen asleep. How she would awaken, Delia didn't know. But for now, there was no potion or cure, no enchanted kiss to free her from the dark spell.

4

Lessons

In the last few minutes of Miss Tupine's class, Madame silently entered the studio. She sat in a chair almost hidden by the piano, but every girl knew she was there. Delia felt Madame watching her as she danced the final combination, a big waltz with tour jetés, sauté développés, and grand jetés. Delia was glad Madame was there to see her. Combinations like this showcased her best qualities as a dancer. Her leaps were high and strong. She sliced through space while the other dancers in her group appeared crowded and timid.

After révérence, Miss Tupine called Delia

over to her and Madame.

"Madame has some good news for you," she said briskly.

"Yes, ees good news. Ees time for you to take Pointes Three. Ees hard class, and you and Claire Acton are youngest girls. Veakest, too. Must vork very hard. But that is true of every dancer, even professional. Thees never changes. Member of corps de ballet, soloist, principal, prima ballerina assoluta, all must vork very hard every day."

Delia wanted to ask her what specifically she should work on, but Madame had already turned away. She left the studio as swiftly and quietly as she had entered. Delia felt numb. She had been praised and criticized at the same time, and it felt strange. It was not what she expected she would feel when she day-dreamed about being moved to Pointes Three. She had imagined she would feel proud.

Students filed out the door, crowding

each other with their bags as they descended the stairs to the dressing room. Claire was waiting for her at the bottom of the stairs. She took her by the hand and pulled her aside for privacy.

"What did Madame say to you? Did she advance you to Pointes Three?" Her face was shining with excitement, and Delia felt lucky to have her as a friend.

"How did you know?" Delia asked.

"That's how it always happens. Madame slips in during the last few minutes of class, then Miss Tupine calls you over and Madame delivers the news."

"It didn't happen like that for you. Didn't she call your mom?" asked Delia. And then a thought formed. *Maybe Madame knows my mother is dead.*

"She did. But you see, she knows my mom. She studied with her for years." Claire went on. "Madame doesn't like talking to moms because they don't know anything about ballet unless they were dancers themselves. All those moms hanging out in the lobby trying to schmooze with Madame are wasting their time. They're probably doing their daughters more harm than good, especially if they're fat. If a girl with a fat mom gains even a tiny bit of weight Madame will send her to Miss Dairy to get weighed in the office. She keeps charts on some girls, you know."

"Weight charts? Are you kidding?" asked Delia incredulously.

"Oh, yes," said Claire. "Things are different in Pointes Three. It's much more professional. She'll give up on you if you gain weight, or, worse yet, she'll get furious and start ridiculing you in front of the class. Last week I saw her pick up the rosin box and pretend to hit Cynthia."

Delia knew who Cynthia was. She was one

of the older sylphs, a strong technician with perfect legs and feet, who had trouble keeping her weight down. Even in the short time Delia had been at the Elanova School, she had noticed Cynthia grow thicker about the waist and hips.

"'Cynthia!' Madame yelled. 'Eef you gain vone more ounce I'm going to beat you vith this box. Vhat are you now? I bet you veigh over vone hundred and fifteen pounds! See Miss Dairy at vonce!'"

"What did she say?"

"She didn't say anything. She burst into tears and left."

The story was worrisome. Delia had never really thought about her weight. Miss Sherrie had told her she had a good build for dancing, and her doctor once said she was naturally thin, but perhaps she wasn't thin enough for Madame. She worried she might gain weight once she started her period. She had seen it happen to some of the girls at school. Girls who had been coltish in grade school became sweaty and plump in junior high. They went to the nurse complaining of cramps, got out of gym, and seemed tired and bored all the time. *If I see that happening to me, I'll stop eating,* Delia vowed.

After putting on her street clothes, Delia went to the office and asked Miss Dairy to call her a cab. She waited in the lobby, sitting in one of the old gilt armchairs near the samovar, staring off into space. She thought of what might be happening at home, her father yelling, Pearl slamming doors, and felt her stomach tighten. *Good*, she thought. *I won't want to eat dinner.*

Down the hall, in the smaller studios to the side of the entrance, a class was about to begin. Delia couldn't tell what type it was. It wasn't modern, jazz, flamenco, or tap. She studied the dancers who clustered near the door. They were teenagers and young adults, middle-aged and older women. An older woman wearing a necklace made of leather and shells and beaded bracelets from her wrist to her elbow tied an orange sarong around her waist. Another woman balanced a baby on her hip as she practiced a confusing little step. A group of men lugged an assortment of strange-looking drums into a studio. One of them wore a "Brasil! World Cup 1998!" T-shirt, and, from the bits of conversation she overheard, she determined it was a Brazilian dance class.

The teacher was tall and toffee-colored, with shoulder-length braids and long feline muscles. He was listening to a smiling young woman with a tattoo of a sunburst on her shoulder. It was only when he laughed that Delia could determine he was a man. It was a deep, husky laugh that rolled and bounced down the hallway. The girl with the tattoo joined in loudly. Delia had never heard anyone laugh like that in the Elanova school before, not even in the dressing room. Miss Dairy stomped out of her office and shushed them. A few moments after she left, the teacher and the girl broke up again, this time into silent giggles.

He caught his breath and said, "Can you believe all the little ballerinas are afraid of her and the crazy Russian lady?" Delia listened carefully. His accent emphasized the percussion of *r*'s and *t*'s and the length of vowels.

The girl shook her head in disbelief.

"It's true! You!" he called to Delia. "Yes, you, little ballerina. Aren't you and your friends afraid of Miss Dairy and Madame?"

"Afraid of Madame?" said Delia. She tried to hide her shyness, but the question came too unexpectedly for her to respond. "What do you mean exactly?"

But the Brazilian and his student had lost

interest. They walked into the studio together laughing again, and Delia wondered if they were making fun of her.

The house was dark and empty when Delia got home. She made herself a cup of chamomile tea and finished her history homework upstairs in her room. Finally, her father and Pearl came home.

There was no screaming or yelling. Mr. Ferri climbed the stairs to his room, passing Delia's open door without a word, and Pearl banged around in the kitchen. Delia went downstairs to see her.

"Hi," she said.

"Hi," said Pearl. Her makeup had been washed off, and she looked tired. She was making macaroni and cheese from a box. She stirred some butter and powdered cheese into a steaming pot on the stove.

"Are you okay?" Delia asked.

"I don't really feel like talking right now."

Pearl settled herself at the breakfast table and turned on the TV. She ate out of the pot with a wooden spoon.

In silence the two sisters watched *Animal Planet*. Wolves were being reintroduced to the wild in Glacier National Park in Montana, and the ranchers, worried about their sheep, were protesting.

"Idiots," muttered Pearl, staring at the screen.

"I better go finish my homework," Delia said finally.

"You go do that, Little Moon." She didn't even look at Delia.

Delia stomped upstairs and shut her door, hating how Pearl was acting, glad to be alone in her room away from her and their father. She put on her pajamas, and crept into bed with her French book. There was a vocabulary quiz tomorrow. She whispered the words and tested herself on their definitions. *Chat*, *tour, poisson* and *tomber* were easy to remember, for there was a ballet step for each word—pas de chat, tour en l'air, temps de poisson, tombé. She loved the music of the language. No wonder it was the language of dance.

She put the book on her bedside table and turned out the light. The softness of her pillow melded with the words in her head. She saw herself dancing in the blue light of a stage and fell asleep.

5

Flour

Now that she was in Pointes Three, Delia entered the doors of the Elanova School with more confidence. She no longer glanced at Madame's portrait every time she passed it, and she wore her hair in a different style, a French twist. After hearing Madame tell one of them she should always wear her hair like this for it enhanced the line of the neck, Delia closed herself in the bathroom with hairspray and pins until she mastered it. She was following one of the other unspoken rules of the school—follow every bit of advice or criticism you hear as if Madame meant it only for you.

She bought a calorie counter and a little postal scale to weigh the portions of her meals, and she began weighing herself every morning. In the dressing rooms, the older girls criticized their hips and thighs, openly envied each other, and traded dieting tips. They glared or winced at themselves in the mirrors. Their chatter about protein and fat grams had convinced Delia that all serious dancers, no matter how naturally thin they were, dieted. She weighed 108 pounds and wanted to weigh 101.

Delia was spending more time at the studio. She raced from school so she could catch the earlier bus and watch the end of the advanced technique class as she stretched. The hour and a half class was full of dance majors from American University and the older sylphs who had obtained release time from school. When they were in ninth grade, the year the D.C. schools allowed it to happen, Delia and Claire planned to do the same. They would get their physical education requirement waived so that they could leave school earlier in the day and take Madame's 3:00 to 4:30 advanced class. It was ridiculous, they agreed, that they had to take P.E. for two more years. Already they were training as much as any varsity athlete, and the P.E. classes were silly and banal—anemic games of field hockey in the blinding sun, tennis matches with poorly strung rackets, Ping-Pong, square dancing. Until then, they would take Miss Tupine's 4:30 to 5:30 class, followed every Monday, Wednesday, and Friday by an hour of Pointes Three with Madame. Their only other class with Madame was the advanced technique class on Saturday morning. But even though they took class from Miss Tupine more often than from Madame, the girls considered Madame to be their true teacher. They were studying with her.

Since her arrest, Pearl had been even more removed from her sister and father. She locked herself in her room for hours at a time. Delia imagined she was reading her books on white

magic and casting spells. Country Day had
agreed to allow her to attend until Mr. Ferri
found a boarding school for her. She did not
skip classes again, but she did not put any
more effort into being on time or earning sat-
isfactory grades either.

Thick envelopes from girls' boarding schools
in New England arrived in the mail. Statements
of philosophies, colored brochures, and admis-
sions forms with centered crests littered Mr.
Ferri's desk. Delia leafed through them when he
was out on a ride one Saturday afternoon. She
read the few lines he had written about Pearl.

*My daughter is exceptionally intelligent but
achieves far below her potential. I believe
this is because she never recovered from the
death of her mother, which occurred when
she was seven. I have tried to be the best
parent I could, but I am convinced that
Pearl needs the structured environment
your school provides.*

A cloud of sadness descended on Delia. It was the first time she could remember her father mentioning the death of their mother. She read the words again and thought of the two of them watching her grow thin and weak. *They needed her*, she thought. *None of this would be happening if she were alive.* Delia carefully replaced the papers on her father's desk, leaving no sign that anyone had been there at all.

"You are spoiled, lazy, and indulged," said Mr. Ferri to Pearl at dinner later in the week. "By the time I was your age, I was working in the bakery six hours a day, twelve on the weekend. You have no comprehension of how lucky you are, how hard I have worked to give you and Delia the opportunities I never had."

Pearl remained impassive. She sat quietly, her hands folded in her lap, her face composed in a non-expression. Every now and then she yawned.

A year ago, when Pearl stole the dough-nuts, there was screaming and slamming doors. Delia lay facedown on her bed, holding a pillow over her head to block out the sound. This was the first argument since Pearl's arrest, and Delia found it easy to ignore. In her mind, she revisited the combination from that afternoon's pointe class, exploring where she could have played with the music or put more softness in her arms. She hummed softly to herself but nobody noticed. She had eaten only a portion of her dinner. Pearl had eaten nothing.

After dinner, Pearl slinked off to her room and locked the door. Their father evaporated into his study. Delia stayed behind to clear the table and load the dishwasher. Not much later, Mr. Ferri came downstairs.

"What's going on with her?" he asked. "Has she said anything to you about leaving Country Day? About going to boarding school? Is she planning to run away?" He stopped himself and looked directly in her eyes. "Is she doing drugs?"

"No, Daddy," replied Delia. "She's not into drugs. She's into nature and myth and spirits and stuff. I don't know what she thinks about leaving Country Day and going to boarding school. She doesn't talk to me about things like that."

"She doesn't talk to me about anything. Go talk to her. See if you can get her to open up a little." He took a plate out of Delia's hand. "Go on. I'll finish this."

Pearl removed the chain lock and let in her sister. She had just finished trimming her bangs. Little bunches of black hair littered the floor.

"Help me clean up," she said.

"Okay," said Delia. She brushed the downy hair into her hand and went to toss it in the wastepaper basket.

"Don't!" yelled Pearl. "I need that." Pearl took the hair and put it in a drawstring bag, opened the window and hung it from the bare branch of a maple tree. She stretched out on

her canopy bed. "What's up?" she asked.

"Dad sent me. He wants me to get you to open up so I can report back to him."

"Typical. Why doesn't he try himself?"

"He says you never talk to him about anything."

"It's true. But then again, he hasn't talked to me in years." Pearl picked up a circle of yarn from her bedside table and began to play cat's cradle. She stared intently at the patterns she made. Delia watched her, feeling useless.

"Do you remember," began Pearl, "when Mom was alive and Dad still worked in the bakery—the old bakery?"

"No," Delia admitted sadly. "I barely remember the old bakery, and I don't remember Mom at all."

"She smelled like flour."

"Flour doesn't have a smell."

"It does. It smells sweet and clean. Daddy used to smell like that before he hired Flavio to manage the bakeries. Dad never really liked the bakery, but Mom did. She loved it there."

Pearl rolled over on her stomach and pulled out a manila envelope from under the mattress. Inside were three faded photographs of their mother. "Do you remember these? They used to hang in the hallway next to our baby pictures."

Delia climbed up on the bed to look. A petite woman in a baker's hat and apron stands with her hands on her hips, smiling at the camera. In the second, a beautiful bride gazes into her bouquet. In the last, the same woman is holding Pearl. They are laughing, and their faces are smudged with flour. Both of them hold up a gingerbread man. Six raisins make a smile.

"I do remember these!" said Delia. She looked at them carefully. "You look so much like her."

"Dad took them down a few years ago. I found them under the blotter on his desk when I was sneaking around his office last summer.

He never noticed they were gone."

Delia shook her head with dismay. "I don't get it. Why did he take them down? Why doesn't he ever talk about her?"

"He doesn't remember her. Or, he blocks her out of his brain on a minute by minute basis. He's good at that." She tapped the photograph of her with her mother, slowly and gently, as if she were sending a code.

"I wish I remembered something about her."

"I wish you did, too, Little Moon. Sometimes I'm lonely. I'm the only one who misses her anymore."

"I miss her, too. In a way," Delia added quickly. She knew it wasn't the same. She couldn't miss her mother in the same way Pearl did.

Delia reported to her father in his office.

"I don't think Pearl is going to run away."

"Good. What kind of mood is she in?"

Delia searched her mind for the most

neutral description she could give. She couldn't possibly tell him that Pearl had just shown her three photographs of their dead mother and was feeling that he had abandoned the memory of his wife.

"I'd say she's quiet."

"Quiet, eh? Good. I think I'll tell her about the Highton School. I think it's the best place for her. It's perfect for Pearl. There are only twelve girls in a class and each student is assigned a horse to train and take care of. There are miles of trails through the campus, a solid college prep program, art studios, and language labs."

"I wouldn't do that right now, Dad. She's not that kind of quiet, more like the 'I want to be alone' quiet."

Relieved that she had convinced her father not to mention the Highton School, Delia got ready for bed. She washed her face, brushed her teeth and hair, and curled up in bed. She lay in the dark trying to conjure up the smell of flour. She could not. It was Pearl's memory, not hers. She was glad her sister had this much of their mother, but she felt empty because she had none of her own. She tossed and turned, and it was some time before she fell asleep.

6

Roses

Days later, on a Friday morning, Mr. Ferri drove Pearl to the Highton School for Girls in Pennsylvania. It was a six-hour drive. Pearl slept most of the way, while Delia, who came along to say good-bye, listened to *Swan Lake* and *Sleeping Beauty* on her Discman. She was attempting to memorize the Petipa choreography and used her hands to dance on the armrest. Her hair was loose and wavy from the braids she slept in the night before. They passed miles and miles of bare trees and empty fields. The gray sky was full of barely visible clouds.

"Are we there yet?" asked Pearl. She had

woken up exactly as the car pulled in to the grand circular driveway of the Highton School for Girls. She rubbed her eyes and blinked at the Georgian mansion before her. In the distance, a few girls on horseback appeared on the hills beyond the main gates.

Delia jumped out and ran to the front door. The classical columns and half-circular entrance porch was a perfect setting for a pose from *Sleeping Beauty*. She struck a balance in attitude just like Aurora in the "Rose Adagio." "This is *so* beautiful!" she laughed. "You're going to love it here, Pearl."

"Little Moon," snapped Pearl, "don't ever make predictions about my feelings." She lumbered up to the entrance with a huge sack on her back and the sewing basket dangling from a curved finger. She dumped them on the porch next to Delia's feet. Delia had an urge to put an arm around her sister, but she stopped herself. She knew Pearl wouldn't appreciate it. Mr. Ferri rang the bell, which seemed to echo down a vast, empty corridor. The headmistress greeted them and showed them into her office.

"Perhaps, Delia, you would like to take a walk in our statuary garden while your father, Pearl, and I get to know each other. Nothing is blooming, of course, but the statues are impressive, well over a hundred years old," she said.

"I'd love to see them," Delia agreed. She nearly bounded down the steps, eager to stretch her legs after the long ride, and get back to immersing herself in the world of Tchaikovsky and Petipa.

The rosebushes were trimmed and bare, and the flower beds dormant, but the old garden was stately and graceful. Two rows of weathered statues surrounded by rosebushes stood on pedestals facing each other across a white path of small, smooth stones. Every now and then, Delia stopped to imitate one. She studied the relation of head to shoulders, what

Madame called épaulement. Even if she was missing class, she could learn something from these crumbling imitations of the great statues of antiquity. After all, as Madame always says, a dancer must learn from all the arts and nature as well. "Even vhen you are not in class, you must find vays to develop your art."

Delia looked around her. A winged Nike stepped into the wind. A laughing Bacchus presented a cascade of grapes. A wounded Amazon, her face stained from the paint of a senior prank, leaned wearily against a column. And there was Mercury leaping into space, his arm and leg in the beautiful S curve of a perfect attitude. Delia mirrored one after another, then danced her way to the next.

It was an old garden. It was an old school, once a prestigious one. But now, as the unkempt grounds and buildings attested, the school had fallen on hard times. Clearly, the Highton School was short of funds, desperate for the donations from the wealthy parents of the troubled girls it educated. *Of course*, thought Delia as she practiced her chaîné turns. *Why else would the Highton School accept Pearl?*

After an hour or so of strolling and dancing through the grounds, Delia intuited it was time to meet Pearl and her dad in the office of the headmistress.

"Well," whispered Pearl in mock surprise, "it looks like she's going to accept me. Can you believe it?" Her face was clear of makeup, and her hair was tied back in a neat ponytail. For the first time in a long while, Delia remembered that Pearl was pretty, and she was filled with a combination of fear and love for her.

"Do you like it here?" Delia asked.

"It's okay. Not any different from any other school, except they have horses. Every girl here has her own horse. Did you see the stables?"

"No. I stayed in the rose garden."

"Oh, yeah. I could see you from the window," Pearl said with a sly expression. "You were dancing with the statues. 'There's Little Moon,' I said to myself, 'off in her own little fantasy world.'"

Delia's stomach burned with irritation. "What's the real world?" she wanted to ask. Getting kicked out of school after school after school? Making Dad stay up all night worrying about you? Hanging out with losers? She didn't ask these things. Finally she said, "And your world is the real one?"

"More real than yours."

Their father and the headmistress joined the girls, laughing in the adult manner Delia, like Pearl, had come to despise.

"I'm sure Pearl will be very happy with us here at Highton School," the headmistress said as she put an arm around her shoulders. Pearl responded with a shockingly false smile that both impressed and frightened Delia with its boldness. "Don't worry about her bags. Two of the juniors will come down to help.

That way Pearl can begin making some friends. Perhaps you, too, Delia might join us here. Your father tells me your grades are excellent."

"No, thank you," Delia said politely. "I'm a very serious ballet student. I have to continue studying with my teacher."

"Yes," replied the headmistress. She fingered her long necklace a bit nervously. "Ballet is a demanding art. But, perhaps you will change your mind."

"I doubt it, although your school is very pretty. I like the statues in the rose garden."

Mr. Ferri said good-bye to the headmistress, kissed Pearl, and reminded her to phone. Delia hugged her sister tightly.

"I miss you," she whispered in Pearl's ear.

"No, you don't," she whispered back. "Nobody does."

But I do, thought Delia as she waved to Pearl from the car window. Her sister stood amidst her luggage and waved back.

In pointe class the following afternoon, Madame entered carrying a single red rose.

"Girls," she began in her most regal tone. "Today I give present to girl most like this rose. Is beautiful, no? Today I vant to see beauty." Occasionally, when Madame made one of her more histrionic pronouncements, Mr. Guest ever so slightly raised his eyebrows. Delia looked to him now, but he sat in his chair as usual, stoic and glum. Using the piano as her barre, Madame demonstrated pliés then asked Mr. Guest for some Schubert.

"What's all this about?" Delia asked Claire between exercises.

"*Nutcracker*'s coming. She's stirring up the competition so she can make up her mind about parts. Age-old Elanova trick."

And class was more demanding than usual. There were dozens of passés, échappés, and coupé développés at the barre. Delia concentrated on connecting her movements to her center and ignored the developing blisters on her feet. Unlike previous weeks, however, Madame gave her no looks of encouragement.

When it was time for the center, Madame moved the girls about like markers. She directed Claire to the center of the second line, an advancement over her usual place at the end. She waved Delia into the far left of the back line with a bored expression on her face. It was the place reserved for the girls who daydreamed at the barre and forgot the combinations. Delia was hurt and confused, unsure of what she had done to deserve such punishment. It unnerved her. She fell out of her pirouettes and slipped during the allegro exercise.

After révérence, Madame presented the rose with a flourish to Claire.

"I give this rose to Claire Acton for her beautiful extension and her hard vork. All of you can learn from this girl."

One by one, the girls took Madame's hand, curtseyed and said their thanks. Madame seemed to merely tolerate Delia's curtsey.

Again, she felt a flush of confusion and shame.

Delia attempted to disappear as quickly as possible, but she nearly ran into Madame as she left the changing room.

"Excuse me, Madame," she uttered.

"Delia!" she said in an angry voice. "Vhy veren't you in class on Friday? Vone girl told me you are in play at school. You cannot be both actress and dancer. I don't have time for girls who vant to be actress."

"No, Madame!" she replied, wondering who would say such a thing. "I'm not in any play at school. I was away on a family trip. My father and I had to drive my sister to her new school in Pennsylvania."

"Dancers do not have time for family trip! Vhy didn't he leave you at home so you can take ballet class?"

"I guess he thinks I'm too young to stay alone."

"Too young? But you are dancer! You are hard vorking, responsible girl! You are not like stupid American teenagers chasing boys and hanging out on street vith cigarettes in their mouths!" She spoke angry Russian to the ceiling and shook her head. Her accent grew thicker. "Next time your father goes avay, you stay vith friend from class. You ask to stay at Claire Acton's house."

"Yes, Madame."

"You are making good progress, Delia. Line of leg, feet, épaulement—all very pretty. But you can't miss any more class. Alvays you must vork very hard. Your technique is not strong enough for your age. You must vork! Vork!" Madame stamped her foot and marched down the hallway. She opened a little door near the office and climbed the stairs to her apartment above the studios.

In spite of the scolding, Delia wanted to follow Madame. She wanted to be one of the girls Madame occasionally invited up for tea. She wanted to see Madame's treasures, the relics and talismans she had inherited from her teachers and her career—the old costumes and photographs, the pointe shoes that belonged to Pavlova and the sketches Nijinsky made while he was choreographing *L'Après-Midi d'un Faun*. She wouldn't miss any more classes. She would strive to keep her focus the entire length of the class. Madame was offering her a rose, too, and it was only barely out of reach.

7

Hands

"No," said Claire to Delia. "It's more like you've just strummed a guitar. Relax your fingers. Lift your elbow."

It was late Friday night. Delia and Claire had interrupted a video of the Bolshoi Ballet performing *Swan Lake* to practice how to hold their arms and hands in arabesque. Delia had long admired how Claire held her hands. The girls studied themselves in front of the mirror in Claire's bedroom.

Delia lifted her leg and arms in first arabesque again. This time she focused on feeling a perfect line of energy flowing from fingertip to fingertip.

"Yes!" said Claire. "Much better! Don't let your thumb drop too much. Great. Now, memorize how this feels."

Delia held the pose trying to memorize exactly how the energy felt through her arms and back.

"Thanks," she said. "That really helped."

"Don't mention it. You looked beautiful. Madame loves your arabesque."

"How do you know?"

"Because you're the only one she looks at when a group does piqué arabesques across the floor. Even when she's watching someone else, she's watching you from the corner of her eye. You know that look she gets."

The girls went to the kitchen to make popcorn. Claire's mother was padding around in her robe, preparing a tray with two cups of chamomile tea.

"Why are you up so late?" asked Claire.

"What do you mean, me? What about you two?"

"We're having a sleep-over. You always stay up late at a sleep-over."

"Of course," replied Mrs. Acton, stirring some honey into the tea. "How silly of me to forget." She looked up and saw Claire shaking the pot back and forth. "Remember, Claire, the best way to stay thin is to always go to bed a little hungry."

"Don't worry, Mom. I'm not putting any butter on it."

"Well, okay . . ." She sighed. She took the tray and left. Her fluffy white slippers made soft sounds down the hallway.

Delia couldn't believe what she had just heard. Claire was lanky as a colt. She had no breasts, and her hips were as straight as a boy's. Delia thought she could lose a few pounds, but certainly not Claire. Secretly, she touched her sternum. She was relieved to feel ribs just under a thin layer of skin.

"My dad never watches movies," said Delia in order to change the subject. She felt embarrassed for her friend.

"Why not?" asked Claire. A burst of steam escaped when she took off the lid to salt the white kernels.

"He doesn't have time. He's too busy with the bakeries and training for the AIDS ride. He is pretty obsessed with cycling right now," Delia went on.

"I wish my dad would exercise," replied Claire, nibbling at a tiny handful of popcorn. "He's fat."

The girls carried their popcorn and diet sodas back to Claire's room and resumed watching *Swan Lake* as they stretched and worked on their turnout.

They slept in late the next morning, and Mrs. Acton had to wake them up for their 10:30 ballet class. Perhaps because of the chill in the November air, Miss Tupine was more animated than usual. There was a brisk allegro combination of jetés battus and tight little pas de chat, and a rousing grand allegro combination across the floor. Mr. Guest played a thundering version of the waltz from *La Traviata* that made Delia break into a smile as she leaped across the room in a grand jeté. She felt airborne and daring, and she laughed at herself for enjoying it so much.

At home, a letter from Pearl waited for her on the bed. It was the first word from Pearl since she had entered the Highton School. There had been no phone calls, no other letters. When Delia opened the envelope, out fell three tiny feathers.

Dear Little Moon,

Stormy here, wind and ice, so I rescued a nest from the rafters outside my window. Don't want momma bird to fly back to a broken home all ready to lay her eggs. I'll put it back when the worst is over. There were six gray feathers inside—three for you and three for me. Hide one in your hair,

*and in class you will soar like a falcon.
That's my spell for you.*

*As for me, I'm using my feathers to
charm my horse, Hades. He's angry and
strong willed, too proud to let me put a
bridle on him. I've pinned a feather to his
stall, buried another halfway between my
room and the stables, and pinned the last
one above my bed. I'm connecting us,
whether he likes it or not.*

Lots of love from your big sister,

Pearl

Delia brushed the three feathers against her
cheek, picturing Pearl at the gray school with
the crumbling statues and sagging verandas.
She worked the feathers into the middle of her
bun and wished both spells would come true.

The house was empty. Her father was still
on his Saturday ride. Delia walked past Pearl's
room, then went back and opened her door.
True to his word, her father had removed the

locks Pearl had installed. Delia sat on her sister's pink bed. Her altar to dead poets and musicians was gone. The closet was nearly empty. There was no circle of blue sand or Spanish shawl. The room looked just as it did when Pearl was a little girl. It wasn't really Pearl's room anymore. It was more of a memorial to the girl her father wanted Pearl to be. How easy it was to make Pearl disappear, Delia thought. All her father had to do was send her away.

The following Monday an air of excitement permeated the lobby of the Elanova School. Girls of all ages clustered around the bulletin board. Little ones jumped up to see better. Older ones looked either jubilant or stricken. One girl dropped her face in her hand and cried. Off to the side the two anorexics, ghostly and pale, watched the girls come and go, their small bright eyes observing all. Delia made her way to the front to see the source of all the commotion. It was the cast list for

Nutcracker written out in Madame's dramatic, flowing hand. Next to it was a typed rehearsal schedule.

Delia scanned the list of parts—Clara, Military Dolls, Favorite Aunt, Friends of Clara, Dancing Doll, Herr Drosselmeyer—finally she found her name listed by the word "Star." Claire Acton's name was listed, too, as well as another name she didn't recognize. "What's that?" she asked herself. She didn't remember any stars in *Nutcracker*.

In the dressing room Claire ran up to her and hugged her with excitement.

"Congratulations!" she squealed. "You're Star! I am, too!"

"Congratulations yourself," Delia answered, hugging her back. "But, what is Star?"

"The star at the top of the Christmas tree. You know the big booming music when the Christmas tree grows? In Madame's choreography, Star comes down from the tree and dances with Clara before she meets the

Nutcracker. It's a beautiful part, and it means we are *destined*!"

"Destined? What do you mean?"

"Only the girls who have a chance of becoming professional dancers get to be Star. The following *Nutcracker* they're usually in 'Mirlitons,' or if they're really strong technically, they might be in 'Tea.' The next year, if they haven't grown too tall or too fat, they'll be a soloist in the 'Waltz of the Flowers,' and the following year, if they're still progressing, and they're still skinny, and they haven't had any major injuries, they get to be the Snow Queen."

"What about Sugar Plum?"

"No," said Claire shaking her head. "No student ever dances Sugar Plum. Madame always asks one of her former students who dances with a European or a New York company to dance Sugar Plum. They were all Star when they were our age. So you see, it's a sign for us. If we work hard, and if we don't get injured or fat we can be professional dancers."

Delia broke into a squeal of excitement, and the two girls jumped up and down hugging each other. A life in the studio. Days that begin with pliés and end with révérence. Chopin and Tchaikovsky, Schubert and Brahms. Train rides through Europe from one baroque opera house to the next, waiting in the wings for an entrance, your body dreamlike and blue from the lights above. A life of dance and art, music, performance, and work—suddenly it was all Delia wanted. It was the first time she could describe the life she wanted for herself, and in the same moment she realized that Claire had been working to attain this life for years.

"How do you know all this stuff?" Delia asked. She hiked up her tights and slipped into her good old, tried and true, black leotard.

"My mom and I have been here forever," she said, and sighed. "Nothing has really changed. As Mother says, 'Only the faces are different.'"

The two girls pinned up the loose ends of each other's hair and walked to the studio. Younger girls and girls their own age who were cast as a Candy Cane or a Friend of Clara seemed to move aside for them.

"A word of warning," whispered Claire as they stretched at the barre. "Expect some jealousy from the others. Don't leave your ballet bag hanging around."

"Will people steal from me because I'm Star?" Delia asked incredulously.

"Absolutely! Madame has set us apart from the others, and she's hurt plenty of feelings with her casting. Just don't be surprised if your new pair of leg warmers suddenly disappears."

And then Delia remembered how someone had told Madame that she was in a play at school. She accepted Claire's comment for the small bitter truth that it was.

Delia took her heel in her hand and stretched her leg to its full extension. She raised her supporting leg to relevé, let go of her leg, and held it well above ninety degrees, her arm in a triumphant fifth position. She practiced relaxing her hand the way Claire showed her. Her fingers gracefully flowed from her palm as if she were strumming the strings of an invisible lute.

8

Ghosts

In the wretched cafeteria of Markham Middle School, Delia sat at a graffiti-riddled Formica table. While she waited for Claire, she wrote a letter to Pearl.

> *Madame gave me a good part in Nutcracker—I'm the star at the top of the Christmas tree that dances with Clara before the Snow Scene. I rotate dancing it with my new friend, Claire Acton.*
>
> *I was thinking about those photographs of Mom you have. I noticed three blank spaces in the hall. You can only see them if the lights are on, and I wonder if that's*

where they used to hang before Dad took them down. By the way, did you take them with you to boarding school? If so, I'd like one for myself, but only if you feel you can spare it.

She composed her sentences between bites of her three-hundred-calorie lunch—carrot sticks, nonfat vanilla yogurt, a rice cake, and a diet soda. She barely heard the students talking and milling about carrying molded trays of bland, greasy food.

Just then Claire collapsed in the chair next to her.

"Sorry I'm late," she said. "I had to stay late to finish a science test. I brought some things to show you . . ." She pulled a dozen or so old programs from performances of the Elanova School from her backpack.

Delia folded the letter and tucked it into her math book. She had been eager to look at them ever since Claire told her about them.

Her mother had taken her to the school's *Nutcracker* and spring performances ever since she had been born.

"Who is that?" Delia asked, pointing to a photograph of a girl in a soaring grand jeté, her legs slightly beyond full splits and her arms in fourth position.

"That," said Claire, chomping on a stick of celery, "is Annalisa. She was so gifted! Perfect legs. Perfect feet. Perfect line. Perfect technique. She was the youngest Snow Queen ever—fifteen. But Madame refuses to say her name. She pretends she's dead."

"Why?" asked Delia.

"Because she left to study in New York when she was sixteen, and it broke Madame's heart. Madame stayed upstairs crying in her apartment for two weeks. When she finally came downstairs, she wore sunglasses to hide her eyes."

"What's so bad about going to New York? I want to go study in New York. I'm even thinking of graduating high school a year early so I can take classes at Ballet Metropolitan's school."

"We all want to study in New York, but don't ever tell Madame."

"Why not?"

"Because she'll think of you as a traitor. She won't tell you that to your face. Instead, she'll tell you to go ahead and leave, or else she'll completely ignore you until you get so depressed and humiliated you have to leave. Madame wants her sylphs to stay with her until they are ready for a professional career. Then she wants to set up private auditions for them with her friends in the companies. She wants to handpick the company for each girl—if you're tall and ethereal with great legs and feet, she'll have you audition at Ballet Metropolitan. If you're more expressive and not so tall, she'll send you to Paris or one of the German companies. That way, she can say to the world, 'Do you see that girl? I trained that girl.' And then, no matter what ballet company you dance with, she will always say you are an Elanova dancer."

"Wow," said Delia. "Madame is *intense*."

"Oh yes," replied Claire. "Intense is the word."

Delia leafed through another program as she took little bites of her rice cake.

"Tell me about her," she said, pointing to a girl in a casual shot in the upstairs studio of the school. She had a playful expression on her face. She stood on pointe behind the barre, her chin resting in her cupped hands with her left leg raised behind her in a fabulous grande attitude. Her lovely, pointed foot was well above her head.

"Oh-h . . ." Claire sighed sadly. "That's Maya. This was taken a year before she fell in pointe class and twisted her knee. I bet she would have danced with Joffrey, but none of the surgeries worked. Her knee was never the same, and she had to give up dancing."

"How awful!" said Delia. She looked carefully at the photograph and saw the light in the girl's eyes. Delia imagined how she might have danced—like a coquette, full of playfulness and mirth.

Claire turned the page. "Look at her," she said.

Delia admired the perfect line of her arabesque. "She's gorgeous," she said. "Great legs and feet. Who is she?"

"I can't remember," answered Claire. "She quit when she was eighteen. Gave up ballet to go to Georgetown and study foreign relations. She threw all her training and talent away."

"What a waste," Delia agreed, shaking her head. It was unimaginable. The girl traded everything Madame had taught her for something so meaningless.

The school day dragged on. Girls looked in mirrors and applied lipgloss. Delia glanced at the notes they passed and regarded their curious, loopy handwriting. Boys read extreme sports magazines and showed each other their collection of CDs. Few listened to the French teacher reciting the list of irregular verbs on tomorrow's quiz, and the teacher did not seem to care. Delia took clear, competent notes, listened to the Chopin playing in her head, and choreographed an adagio for herself.

She walked to the bus lost in dreams of ballet. She saw herself auditioning in New York with a number pinned to her back, dancing before a table of Russian teachers and retired ballerinas. She saw herself dancing the mad scene in *Giselle*, pulling petals from a flower, then reaching for the prince's sword. She saw herself being showered with roses from above, and swaddled in leg warmers and a huge sweater at the barre the next morning. She thought of all the girls in the programs—the ones who were gifted, the ones who were injured, the ones who became famous, and the ones who gave up. She thought of how they haunted the Elanova School with their stories, giving caution or inspiration, sympathy or envy to all of the girls who studied with Madame. *I'll have my story,* Delia thought, *for I am Star at thirteen.*

Delia changed quickly in the dressing room and slipped into the upstairs studio to watch the last few combinations of the advanced class. She sat under the baby grand piano and peeked out. The first group was executing the allegro, a wicked combination full of little jumps and beats. There were jetés battus, sissonnes and prise volés, steps that needed clarity, intelligence, and speed. Cynthia looked sleek and thin. She was the only one in her group to perform all the beats and keep to the music. It was a good day for her. She was fast, musical, and precise, and Madame praised her.

"Yes, Cynthia! You like racehorse today! You keep looking and dancing like this and you vill be Snow Queen for opening night of *Nutcracker*."

Delia felt a rush of pride and relief for her

favorite dancer. Opening night of *Nutcracker* was always reviewed in the *Washington Post*, and special attention was given to the Snow Queen and the soloists in the "Waltz of the Flowers," the rising stars among Madame's students. The dance critic frequently made predictions about the future careers of Madame's best dancers. Delia wanted Cynthia to get that attention. She felt a secret bond with her. Their response to music and movement were so similar. She respected the other sylphs, but the only one she felt affection for was Cynthia. Most of the older girls were so serious and glum. Delia watched them warming up, taking class, walking to and from the changing room—the two anorexics emptying packets of sweetener into their instant coffee, the high school girls lugging their ballet bags, the older girls who weren't in college or New York taping their blisters, killing time at the Elanova School between the next round of company auditions. She wondered what happened to them, and if they had ever really loved to dance.

When the men's group, traditionally the last group to dance a combination, took the floor, Delia was surprised to see the Brazilian teacher. He danced barefoot in loose batik pants and an orange sleeveless tank top. His dreds were pulled into a long, thick ponytail. His turnout was poor and his feet weren't fully pointed, but his jumps were buoyant and exact, nailing the music. He sliced the air, making even the more technical dancers seem like plodders. Between groups he remained in the back of the studio stretching his Achilles at the barre, talking to no one. Delia couldn't imagine what he was doing there. Clearly he was a dancer, but not a ballet dancer.

"Is that a man or a woman?" whispered Claire. She had sneaked into the studio and sat next to Delia under the piano.

"It's a man. He's the Brazilian teacher," replied Delia.

"For that adult class?"

"Yeah," said Delia.

"He's weird," said Claire. "Good, in a way, but weird."

"I like his dancing," said Delia, then added, "Why do you think he's taking Madame's class?"

"I bet he's dancing the pas de deux in the Arabian Dance. Madame always has to find some guy outside of the studio for that piece."

"Madame told Cynthia she might dance Snow Queen opening night. If she keeps her weight down," reported Delia.

"She won't," replied Claire. "I've seen her gain and lose that same ten pounds for years."

"Good afternoon, my Stars!" Madame called to Delia and Claire. The advanced class had bowed and clapped and were lumbering out of the studio. "Soon ve begin our first rehearsal!" Madame glowed. She looked exactly as she did in the thirty-year-old photograph of herself dancing the lead in *Coppélia*.

A girl rose from the chair next to the piano and went to talk to Madame. She was probably twelve, and she stood in a casual fourth position, her hands clasped loosely behind her back like a figure in a Degas painting. Her hair was pulled into a large, tight bun and covered with a hair net. Even in the enormous sweatpants belted around her waist, Delia and Claire could tell she had the long, tapered legs Madame loved.

"Delia, Claire, come here, darling girls," sang Madame. "This is Allegra, a new student who just moved to Washington. She came all the vay from Florida to study vith me. She lives vith the family of one of the little girls in Pointes Vone, but I think she needs friends her own age."

Claire rose to the occasion. "We're happy to meet you."

"Allegra is prodigy. *Pro-di-gy! Wunderkind*, they say in Europe. Her pirouettes and leaps like prima ballerina! And she has very smart mother who does not vant her to go to New York until much, much later. Here at Elanova School ve have better training than at company schools and ees better place for young girl. More friendly. Not so harsh. Ees true, no?"

"Very true," answered Claire.

"Oh yes," Delia chimed in.

"Yes! You see, Allegra? You vill like it here, and these two darling girls. They also dance Star." And then she pivoted sharply to face Delia directly and said, "Delia, sveet girl, you must buy new pointe shoes. I vatch your feet in class last veek, and you are not standing on toes. A leetle back, not all the vay on top of toes. Because of this your legs never look straight. You dance like old lady vith gout. Go to Theater Arts and ask Mrs. Vhite to help you find perfect shoe for your feet."

"Yes, Madame," said Delia. "I'll go right away."

"Good girl." With that, Madame swept off, her skirt billowing slightly with her swift exit. The three girls remained facing each other. The new girl wore a tiny, satisfied smile.

Fear and embarrassment descended on Delia, and she did not know what to say to her friend or the new girl. A single, panicked thought sprang to her mind. She had to get her dad to buy her new pointe shoes before the first Star rehearsal. The silence in the room was excruciating, and she was glad when Claire finally spoke up.

"So you're dancing Star, too?" asked Claire.

"Yes," said Allegra in a southern accent. It was a little girl's voice. "Madame says I'm dancing opening night. I'm so excited!"

"Oh," said Delia and Claire together. They looked at her white face and her Popsicle blue eyes. They were slightly slanted. Not a strand of her light blond hair was out of place.

"Would you like to come stretch with us?" Delia offered.

"No, thank you. I need to get some water

before class." Allegra nearly skipped out of the studio, secure and unimpressed, as if the Elanova School had forever been her personal domain.

"I bet her eyes are slanted like that because she pulls her hair so tightly," said Claire.

"Why does she get opening night?" complained Delia. They sat facing each other, massaging each other's Achilles tendons and glowering. She was glad that Claire's jealousy left no room to delve into Madame's comment about her dancing like an old lady with gout.

"She must be good," Claire spat out. "Really good. I've never heard Madame call someone a prodigy before."

And Allegra was really good. Miss Tupine nearly drooled over her extension at the barre. She had her demonstrate how to lift the leg over the hip in grand rond de jambe en l'air.

"Watch Allegra, girls! See how she lifts the leg even higher as she rotates it from second to arabesque! Beautiful, Allegra. Exquisite!"

Delia imitated Allegra as best she could, but her jealousy got in the way. She felt like yelling at the new girl and wondered what it would take to make her go back to Florida or off to New York.

"There's a new girl in class," Delia grumbled at her father in the car. Usually she said nothing about class, but the bitterness she felt bubbled up to the surface.

"And who's that?" asked her father.

"A prodigy named Allegra."

"A prodigy! Hmmm. . . . Am I detecting some jealousy in my favorite ballerina?"

"I'm not a ballerina. Not yet, anyway. And I'm not jealous. I just hate . . ." Delia thought about what to say. "I hate being replaced."

"Did Madame give her your part?" His eyes stayed on the dark road, but Delia could feel he was trying to help.

"Not exactly. Claire and I are still doing Star, but Madame told her she gets to perform opening night. I can tell Madame is going to give her all her attention. She's the best dancer I've ever seen, she's better than most of the older girls in Pointes Three."

"So she's someone to compete with. That's okay. There will always be someone better than you. It's not a bad thing to realize. Otherwise you're just a big fish in a small pond, always thinking you're the best."

"That really doesn't help, Dad, but thanks anyway." She didn't talk again until they got home.

She declined dinner, lying that she had eaten a huge snack before ballet and felt sick to her stomach. She shut herself in her room and did some homework. Hunger flashed in her stomach and made her light-headed. She told it to go away and let her study her French.

Eventually the light-headedness turned into a headache. It became so bad that Delia had to take some ibuprofen. On her way back from the bathroom, she stopped to look at the three faint rectangles where the photographs of her mother used to hang. She thought of how easy it was for her father to forget her mother and to pretend that Pearl no longer existed. She thought of Madame and how quickly she could shift her attention from one girl to another. Claire could do it, too. She couldn't remember the name of that beautiful dancer who quit ballet for college. She touched the blank space on the wall, and for a second she thought she might faint. She went to bed hungry, determined that she would not give Madame a reason to forget her.

9

Thread

A letter from Pearl crossed with her own in the mail, so there was no mention of the photographs of their mother. Instead, Pearl wrote of her horse, Hades, the horse the headmistress had assigned her. Delia read it in the car while her dad drove her to the dance supply store. Enclosed was an ink drawing of the black horse rearing and kicking his front legs.

> *Dearest Little Moon, little sister,*
> *This is my horse Hades. When I first met him, he stomped the ground, tossed his head and kicked the gate to his stall. The*

riding teacher said that no girl has ever
been able to train him, so of course, I
am committed to being the one to do it.
For two weeks I had to stay ten feet away
from his stall and talk to him in a soft
voice. Now he lets me feed him carrots
and sugar cubes. Sometimes he lets me
pet his neck, but I'm too afraid to pet
his nose. I tried to a few days ago and
he bit my fingers, not hard enough to
break them, but enough to bruise them
pretty badly.

Other than that, not much is going on
here, except that I'm embroidering a
beautiful pillowcase for you. I work on it
late at night when I feel lonely as the
miller's daughter, shut away to spin straw
into gold. Lucky for me, I like the feel of
needle and thread. These are the colors
I'm using.

Love,
Pearl

Snips of blue, green, and violet thread were taped to the bottom of the letter. They blended into each other like the colors of the sea.

Delia finished the letter and put it in her coat pocket. She felt sad. Her sister was lonely. Delia looked down at the Potomac River as they crossed Chain Bridge into Virginia. Gray water rushed between muddy banks, drowning rocks and fallen trees.

"I'm glad you and Pearl are writing each other," said her father.

"So am I," said Delia. She turned on the radio and began dancing with her hands to an intermezzo by Brahms.

"Does she sound happy?"

"I wouldn't say she sounds happy . . . but she loves her horse and she's working hard at training him."

"Good," he said, turning into the parking lot. The music stopped when he turned off the car. He didn't ask anything else about Pearl or her letter, and Delia felt herself grow sullen.

Maybe he just doesn't care about Pearl, she thought. She opened the door to Dance and Theater Arts and her breath became a small white cloud that disappeared.

She and her father passed long glass cases of tiaras and headdresses and went upstairs to the dance section of the store. Delia could tell by the way her father followed that he felt out of place.

Mrs. White was not at all what Delia expected. She was portly and pink faced, in a huge white blouse that hung over her hips, stone-washed blue jeans, and running shoes. Her dark hair was pinned on top of her head in an elaborate style of stacked curls that were sprayed to a crisp. She took deep, wheezy breaths as she carried stacks of slender shoe boxes back and forth.

"I'm surprised I haven't met you before, Delia," she said in a welcoming voice. "Madame sends all her sylphs to me." Delia was relieved. She could tell immediately that

Mrs. White was a kind person.

"I've only been studying with Madame since the summer. She sent me to you because she says I'm not standing right in my pointe shoes."

"Only since June and Star in *Nutcracker*! Madame must like your dancing very much. Now, what pointe shoe have you been wearing? And what size?"

Delia mentioned a brand of American shoes, and Mrs. White threw her head back and laughed.

"Well that's half the problem right there! Madame hates American shoes, says they're unsightly. Even if they fit you perfectly, Madame will find something wrong. No, no, no. No American shoes for an Elanova dancer. Point your foot for me, Delia. We'll try an English shoe, Freed or Gamba. I'll bring them both out for you to try." Mrs. White waddled off, huffing a bit, and chuckling.

A few moments later, Mrs. White returned

with six boxes of pointe shoes—three pairs of Gambas and three pairs of Freeds. Mr. Ferri, finished with his amble about the store, sat down next to Delia on the bench. The Gambas had high vamps and a small pointe. She slipped them on, rose in sous-sous, and did a few échappés. They looked beautiful on her feet, but the small pointe made it difficult to balance. The Freeds were sturdier but less flattering.

"Yes! It's the Gambas for sure," advised Mrs. White. "Margot Fonteyn wore Gambas. Just sew on the wide ribbon for more support. You'll get used to the small pointe quickly. Your ankles are strong. Try on the other two pairs, and we'll see which one is the prettiest."

"Aren't they all the same?" asked Mr. Ferri.

"Oh, no," answered Mrs. White. "Now you listen, too, dear. This is something a girl who dances Star in the Elanova Ballet should know. Look carefully at the soles of these three pairs of Gambas. Do you see those three Xs printed into the leather? Now look at this pair. See the Vs? Those are the signature marks of the shoemakers. Each one has his own mark. Professional dancers know their favorite shoemaker and order directly from them."

"How interesting!" said Mr. Ferri. "A real craft, isn't it?" He picked up each pair and looked at the different marks. It was the sort of thing he appreciated, and Delia wondered if it made him miss working in the bakery like he used to.

"Oh, yes!" said Mrs. White. "Craftsmen indeed. It passes on from generation to generation. Most of their fathers and grandfathers made pointe shoes. Now Delia, try them on. Let's see which pair suits you best."

Delia tried on each pair. She rose on pointe in fifth position in front of the mirror. She tried a few piqués passés and bourréed back and forth. Each was slightly different, but one pair clearly fit her feet the best. They supported her arch and gently held her toes. It was easy to roll up on pointe. The mark on the shank was a double X.

"They should fit like a glove," said Mrs. White. "Are these the ones? Go up on pointe again for me. Are you sure they aren't too wide? Let me see." Mrs. White felt the bones of her ankle to make sure Delia's feet were straight. "Very good. Yes, Madame will like these. Your feet look very pretty."

"Is there anything else you need?" her father asked. "Tights? A new leotard?" He waited for Delia's response before writing out the check. His generosity made Delia feel tender for him, but she also felt slightly guilty. She wondered when was the last time he showed so much interest in Pearl.

"I'm fine, Dad."

"I'm proud of my little star. We'll have to give Mrs. White a photo of you in your costume for that wall."

"No, Dad! That's tacky." Madame would

highly disapprove. Delia pictured her stomping her foot and saying something like, "Ballet is not a talent show!"

Mrs. White rolled out lengths of elastic and ribbon from two enormous pink spools next to the register. She put them in the bag with the pointe shoes.

"Good-bye, dear. Dance well for Madame."

The atmosphere of the Elanova School on Saturday afternoons was even more serious than usual. The older girls were even more aloof. They sat near the piano, sewing pointe shoes or knitting, watching all, silently waiting for Madame to rehearse their part. No one dared to stretch at the barre or on the floor. Madame needed to view the studio as a stage, and there was to be no clutter of any sort. A pair of leg warmers draped over the barre could make her furious.

When Delia arrived at the studio for her three o'clock rehearsal, Claire was already there sitting just outside the door. She quietly described the rehearsal taking place. Madame was still working with the soloists in the Snow Scene. The three girls who were to alternate dancing Snow Queen were in pointe shoes and rehearsal tutus. Five other girls, all strong technicians, were also there. They were the Flurries, the first ethereal creatures Clara sees on her trip through the Land of the Snow to the Kingdom of the Sugar Plum Fairy. Miss Dairy waited by the ancient record player. Her thick glasses magnified her brown eyes to an extraordinary size.

Madame was rehearsing the two anorexic girls. For some reason, she had choreographed a short duet for the pair. They danced to Madame's singsong counting, their bodies spiraling in sauté turns. The artificial flowers one had pinned in her hair went flying across the studio. Delia asked Claire how Madame could dare to put them on stage. Both looked like they might collapse from starvation at any moment. The outline of their sternums were visible through their leotards. Their back muscles rippled like taut strings when they raised their arms.

"Madame is rewarding them for their discipline," Claire said. "Besides, they won't look that skinny on stage. Stage lights add at least ten pounds."

Claire's remark made Delia look down at her waist. She had been going to bed slightly hungry for over a week, and the thin layer of baby fat she used to carry there had almost disappeared. The top of her hip bones was clearly visible through her leotard, but was she thin enough? The thought of Madame saying she was too fat in front of others was unbearable. *I'd want to die,* thought Delia, and she looked again at the anorexics and thought perhaps they weren't too thin after all. In a different place in the world they would look ill, but in the ballet world, their emaciation won them both Madame's attention and immunity from the public humiliations she inflicted upon girls like Cynthia.

Allegra entered the hall but did not sit with the girls. She smiled curtly, walked to the other end of the hall, and rifled through her ballet bag.

The rehearsal of the Snow soloists drew to a close. Madame thanked them and waved them away. With the tension over, the older girls broke into a chatter. Some joked as they collected their things. Others drifted silently to the dressing room. Madame told Delia, Allegra, and Claire to put on their pointe shoes and sent the loyal Miss Dairy to fetch her some tea. Delia felt slightly sick as she put on her new Gambas. Inside her head she told herself to straighten her knees and stand right on the tips of her toes, over and over.

"Darlings," Madame began, her voice weakened by a hint of laryngitis, "you are my Stars. This is beautiful part, most beautiful part after Sugar Plum and Snow Queen. To dance this, you must be very, very alive. All of body and face must scintillate like stars in blackest Russian night. Vhen I play music for you, you listen and vatch. Then you do steps."

Miss Dairy handed Madame her tea, served the Russian style in a glass with a dainty silver holder. She took a few sips and cleared her throat. "Alvays, vhen I hear this music, I remember my years at the academy. This vas my first solo. I had left home two years before to study vith the greatest teachers in Russia. How small my vorld vas! There vere only the studio and the theater, the gray rooms vhere we slept, our footsteps in the snow, no mother to tuck us in at night . . ."

For a few moments Madame was lost in memory. Delia looked at her faraway expression and thought that Madame must have been lonely at times. Finally, Madame shook her head. "Dairy, please," she said finally. "Play Star music for these beautiful girls."

Like true magic, the music was both compelling and frightening. The strings trembled and flashed. Each repetition of the melody grew louder. It seemed to be warning Clara of the dangers she would encounter in the adventure she wanted so badly.

"You are hidden behind presents under tree like this." Madame demonstrated the pose. She lay folded over her beautiful right leg while resting on the other folded behind her. Her head was bowed, and her arms reached toward her right foot. Her hands were full of poetry and grace, as alive as flowers, and Delia wondered if this could be learned, or if each dancer's hands were as unique as snowflakes.

"You listen, listen, listen to music of tree growing to ceiling of parlor, and then vhen you hear the French horn go like this—*BA-BUM*—you know the cymbals are coming. Vhen they crash, you open up like this. Now listen, the cymbals are soon . . ."

With the resounding crash, Madame lifted

her arms and body. Perfectly synchronized to the cymbals, her hands flicked open from the traditional fifth position, and her face lifted into the beam of an invisible spotlight.

"Now, girls, you do it. I vant to see entire body open, dramatic like star bursting through dark night. Is simple, but is not a leetle step. Is *big*! *Grand!* Like entrance of Black Svan in act three of *Svan Lake*—dramatic!"

So taken by the music, Delia was unaware of the others as she imitated Madame. Her heart pounded fast and steady as she counted the music, and she lifted her body and opened her hands in perfect time with the crash of the cymbals.

"*Yes, girls! Yes!!* Now ve go on. . . ."

The choreography was passionate and strong with arms and legs pulling away from each other in the fluorescent tension of a star. There were slow pirouettes in attitude and a string of piqué turns with lifted arms.

"The purpose of this dance," Madame told

them, "is to cast a spell on Clara, to lure her to a life change. The Star does this vith her brilliance. Every move must be sharp and precise."

Delia dove into an arabesque penché on pointe. Her left leg was behind her edging into splits, her right arm reaching to the floor as she balanced on the tip of her right toe. She felt as illuminating and powerful as a laser.

"Yes, Delia!" Madame Elanova cried out. She ordered Miss Dairy to stop the music and then rehearsed the girls in the different areas that gave them trouble. Allegra was told to slow down in the attitude turns and stop trying for doubles. Claire was told to reach more in her arabesque penché, to call out to Clara with her arms instead of looking at the floor as if she had "lost dime on floor of bus."

"And, you, Delia, must turn faster in piqué turns, but feet and legs are perfect—sharp as swords. You have new shoes, yes? You vearing Gambas, now, eh? Ees good pointe shoes for you. Never, never vear different type."

For a moment Delia felt she might cry with relief. But she stopped herself and gave the short smile she had been practicing alone. It expressed a polite self-assurance, a quality Delia craved in the world of prodigies and sylphs where she now found herself.

After rehearsal, Delia had a costume fitting. She descended the stairs to the basement of the school, the storage area for the sets and props, the portable barres and the lost and found. There in the back was a sewing machine and a huge worktable. Surrounded by bolts of satin and tulle and racks of tutus was the costume mistress, Miss Alexandra. She was a tiny, withered old woman who spoke mostly Russian. Her back was stooped as if for years she had been carrying a great burden. She was Madame's sister.

"You Star, no?" she asked, peering into Delia's face. She wore a padded bracelet stuck with pins and a necklace of measuring tape. A few sequins stuck to her neck and the back of her hand.

"Yes, Miss Alexandra," Delia answered. She cast her eyes about the place, itching to try on all the different costumes and to explore the crumbling sets stacked against the wall.

Miss Alexandra handed her a body suit festooned with sequins. She motioned for her to change behind the Chinese screen off to the side. There was a web of glittery fabric between the arms and body, and a headpiece shaped like a point. Delia slipped it on, and her head and limbs were transformed to the five points of a star. When she emerged, Miss Alexandra had Delia stand on a little stool.

"Yah, ees OK," said Miss Alexandra. She circled her hand indicating for Delia to turn around. It was a strange, otherworldly costume. It flashed and shimmered like an opal when it caught the light of the bare bulb above Miss Alexandra. Delia loved it.

"Do you think there are enough sequins?"

Delia asked, noticing how so many were loose and how others fell off as she moved.

"No understan," she muttered, pins in her mouth. She tilted her head, sizing up the work to be done, then began sewing the web of fabric where it had torn away from the leotard.

"I-think-there-need-to-be-more-sequins," said Delia slowly, enunciating each syllable. She looked down and watched the old woman's hands at work.

"I no understan' Eenglis." Miss Alexandra sighed heavily as she bent down to stitch, as if the great curve in her back were a weight pressing down on her heart. "Don't vorry, leetle girl. I vill make you beautiful."

10

Preparation

Delia buried her head in her notebook, brainstorming her list of assignments, tests, classes, and rehearsals for the week. It was Monday, the first day of a long week, the last week before winter break and the opening night of *Nutcracker*. While her history teacher, Mr. McGrath, was setting up a video, she made out a schedule.

Monday: 4–5:30 ballet class
             5:45–6:45 pointe class
             study for history test on Wed.
             work on Solar Energy report—
             due Fri!

Tuesday: 4–5:30 ballet class
              5:45–6:30 Star rehearsal
              study for history test

Wednesday: 4–5:30 ballet class
              5:45–6:45 pointe class
              6:45–7:30 Star rehearsal
              work on Solar Energy report

Thursday: 4–5:30 ballet class
              5:45–6:45 rehearsal for Star
              finish Solar Energy report

Friday: LAST DAY OF SCHOOL!
              4–10 dress rehearsal at theater

Saturday: 8 p.m. OPENING NIGHT!!

She was so engrossed in what she was doing that she did not notice Mr. McGrath looking over her shoulder while the rest of the class watched.

"When do you eat?" he asked incredu-lously. The class laughed, and Delia's face turned red. She was, at that moment, very hungry although she would not have admitted it. She wanted to look her best for her per-formance. Remember, she told herself again and again, stage lights make everyone look ten pounds heavier. Mr. McGrath looked at her with a kind expression. He had not wanted to embarrass her in front of the class. "The next time any of you complain about not having enough time to do your homework, I'm going to have Delia make out a schedule for you. Now, I want you to pay close attention to the section on the Pueblo Indians in this film. Believe me, this material *will be* on Wednes-day's test."

At the end of class Mr. McGrath called Delia to his desk.

"So, is this *Nutcracker* the sort of thing my five-year-old daughter would like? Are there fairies? Soldiers? Princesses?"

"Oh, yes," said Delia. She liked Mr. McGrath. Most of her classmates thought his passion for Native Americans made him a bit odd, but Delia appreciated him. *He's like I am. Inspired.* "There's even a magic Christmas tree and a dancing star."

"Sounds great. Can you get me three tickets? Tickets for a night you're dancing?"

"Sure. I'm Star."

"Star? Did you say you're the star?"

"No!" Delia laughed and shook her head. "I'm not *the* star. I dance the *role* of Star, the star at the top of the Christmas tree."

"Oh, that star! I get it. Well, you're the star I want to see, so get me three tickets ASAP for the night you're dancing."

"I'm dancing Christmas Eve. Is that all right?"

"Sure! Sounds perfect, perfect family outing for Christmas Eve. Okay, then. Here's some money. Bring me those tickets sometime this week. And, hey, try to eat, okay? You're looking kinda boney. And get some sleep. I'm gonna send a child labor activist down to that ballet school of yours!"

All week Delia lugged around an extra heavy ballet bag to and from the Elanova School. It was full of schoolbooks and the extra pointe shoes she needed for Star rehearsals. The only way she could get all of her homework done was to bring it to rehearsals and use every spare moment to read or study. She was discreet about it, sitting just outside the door of the studio, setting out only one book at a time. Madame did not like to be reminded that her students had lives outside ballet.

With all the rehearsals and costume fittings, the atmosphere at the Elanova School was frenzied and tense. Madame was prone to even more tirades than usual, and the dressing room was always echoing with the soft sobbing of at least one humiliated girl. Photographers drifted in and out taking pictures of rehearsals and costumed soloists, and Miss Dairy was perpetually at the copy machine. One draft of the program had already been discarded. Delia was stretching in the foyer, waiting for class to begin, when she overheard Madame screaming about the biography the Brazilian teacher had submitted for himself.

"Vhy can't he just say he danced vith Ballet Nacional do Brasil? Vhy must he include he is priest in ignorant religion?"

"You'll insult him if you make him change it, Alicia," pleaded Miss Dairy. "Remember, his classes are popular and they help pay our bills . . ."

"I don't care!" yelled Madame, stamping her foot. "I von't have this in my program for *Nutcracker*." She threw a pile of papers to the floor, and stomped upstairs to her apartment. A few of the programs floated into the foyer. Delia picked it up and read, stumbling over the pronunciation of his name.

MEIA NOITE began dancing in Candomble rituals in his native Bahia, Brazil, before he could talk. At sixteen he became his village's priest of Ochumare, god of life and change. A year later, he began his professional career by dancing with Brazil's leading folklore company, Ballet Nacional do Brasil. He has toured extensively in Europe, and has performed and choreographed major works in Japan, Hong Kong, and Singapore.

"May-uh Noy-chay. May-uh Noy-chay," she whispered, practicing the name. She was intrigued, for it seemed an odd thing that dance was part of his religion. How did he learn the steps? Did a priest teach him? Did he make it up himself the way you make up a prayer? Maybe his religion was what she saw when she watched him dance, for he had something that she could not put into words. She saw it when he took class and rehearsed. He did not have a lot of ballet technique. But he had energy and boldness, and his port de bras seemed to come straight up out of the floor and through his body. And there was something else, something liquid and mysterious in the way he moved. Delia loved watching him do something as simple as walk across the floor. She stuffed two of the discarded programs into her ballet bag, planning to mail one to Pearl with her next letter. She thought her sister would find Meia Noite interesting.

Dress rehearsal was held in the big art deco theater of one of the universities in town. There were great sweeping staircases and a painted ceiling of deer and nymphs gamboling about. There were dressing rooms with mirrors bordered by makeup lights, an orchestra pit, a green room, catwalks, rows of lights with gels of all different colors, and a slinky black theater cat named Cyrano. Touring dance and theater companies regularly performed there.

Delia and Claire burst out laughing the first time they opened the door at the side of the theater labeled ARTISTS' ENTRANCE.

Before dress rehearsal began, all the soloists and members of the corps de ballet for the Snow Scene and the "Waltz of the Flowers" met onstage for a makeup lesson. The teachers were two of the older sylphs. Seniors in high school, they had trained with Madame since they were little girls. Both were dancing Snow Queen this season. The brunette was, as Claire would say, destined. In the spring she would go to New York to make the rounds of company auditions. The other girl would attend one of the artsy colleges in New England and major in dance. Even though her technique was excellent, her legs were not long enough nor her feet arched enough to be accepted by a professional company. Despite these limitations, she was clearly one of Madame's favorites. Whether it was in fouetté turns, arabesque, or grand jeté, her placement was perfect. She completely embodied all of Madame's teachings, the legacy of form and line that she passed down from the great Russian teachers of her youth. It was a pity about her body, the mothers on the couch often whispered. Yet Madame had great plans for her. The gossip among the mothers, gossip Delia heard one day while resting in splits and waiting for her class, was that she would return upon graduation from college to teach the children's ballet classes. Later, once Madame retired, she would take over the studio and become artistic director of the school. To Delia, she seemed unusually content for an Elanova dancer. She was never one to cry or whine in the dressing room. Instead she seemed to watch the drama about her with an amused detachment. It was she who gave the girls their makeup lesson. She demonstrated on the brunette, who sat on a tall stool facing the semicircle of dancers.

"All Dolls, Stars, Snowflakes, and Flowers

must wear a very pale base. See Mrs. White at Theater Arts if you're not sure if you have the right shade. Dot your entire face, way up to your hairline, like this. Then, blend the dots together with a little sponge . . ." The girl destined for New York sat impassively as her face was painted. "Everyone except the dolls wears false eyelashes. Don't use your fingers to spread on the glue or you'll get it all over the place. Use a Q-tip. Put them on from the inside corner of the eye outwards. It's not as hard as it looks. All dolls should draw five upper lashes with a black pencil. Don't use brown. The point is to make your eyes stand out from a distance."

Delia, Claire, and Allegra sat next to each other, watching and listening carefully. Allegra double-checked her makeup kit with the two Snow Queens. Then the three girls went downstairs to their dressing room to put on their makeup and costumes. Because she was to dance opening night, the night the reviewers came, only Allegra was to dance onstage for dress rehearsal. During the music, Delia and Claire were to rehearse in costume backstage with Miss Tupine.

Once they were dressed and made up, all the dancers in act one assembled backstage. Clara, Fritz, and the friends of Clara, all dressed in Victorian party clothes, wrestled thumbs and played scissors, paper, rock. The military dolls and the dancing doll admired one another's painted eyelashes, and the mice and soldiers chased each other about until Miss Tupine stamped her foot and demanded quiet. Off to the side, patient and professional, the older girls warmed up at the portable barre. Their long white tutus were made of tulle, the finest net, light as thistle down. Delia and Claire practiced their solos for each other and marveled how their opalescent costumes glittered in the glow of the stage lights. In the series of chainé turns, Delia felt herself become a bit of the night sky, the stars from

Madame's Russian childhood, the moon of her name, something celestial and pure. *Yes*, Delia thought, *this is what I want*.

The orchestra was a motley presence in the pit below. Dressed in sweatsuits and jeans, ratty sweaters and old jackets, they talked softly among themselves, waiting to begin, while Madame continued to rehearse Cynthia and her partner. Delia crept to the wings to watch the pas de deux. The choreography was perfect for Cynthia, Delia thought. It highlighted the long lines of her limbs, the regal quality of her shoulders and neck. Delia was unaware that she stood next to Meia Noite. He nudged her gently with his elbow.

"The old woman is torturing that beautiful girl," he whispered. "And she is one of the few real dancers in the school."

"Oh, no," whispered Delia. She was surprised he talked to her.

"The old woman cares only how the body looks. She is blind to the spirit of this girl.

And this girl is one with the saints. I see it in her hands when she dances."

Even though she could never have said those words herself, Delia knew what Meia meant about Cynthia. It named the beauty she saw in the other girl's dancing. Delia edged closer to Meia Noite, and together they watched her from the wings.

Cynthia and her partner were having problems in the opening lift, the sequence when the Snow Queen runs to her cavalier, who lifts her in arabesque high over his head, his arms fully extended. They attempted the lift several times until the cavalier was clearly exhausted. Madame's eyes glistened with anger.

"I just can't get her up!" her cavalier whined. "She's not jumping enough!"

"Cynthia, you must jump! *Jump!* Vhat is trouble? You eat too many Christmas cookies? You able to fasten costume? Turn around. Let me see." Tears black with eyeliner began to run down Cynthia's face. Humiliated, she obeyed. Madame's voice thundered through the empty auditorium. Backstage, silence descended upon the entire cast. Some girls made eye contact and grimaced. Others returned to the dressing rooms. The two anorexic girls, both wearing bulky sweaters over their Snow Flake costumes, continued to warm up at the barre, their concentration unbroken.

Miss Dairy, clipboard in hand, pen behind an ear, clunked across the stage in sensible shoes to interrupt Madame's raging. She touched her gently on the elbow and reminded her that the orchestra was ready to begin. If dress rehearsal did not begin right away, she was going to have to pay them overtime.

"Thees ees not my fault, Dairy!" Her accent was thick with disgust. "Thees ees fault of girl who can't say *nyet* to Christmas cookies! Thees ees fault of girl who loves cookies more than ballet! In Russia, girl like thees is thrown out of academy! Make room for other girl who loves ballet more than food!"

Once again, the cavalier and the barely composed Snow Queen attempted the lift. Miraculously, it was successful. Delia sighed with relief.

"Bravo!" whispered the Brazilian teacher. "Now maybe the old witch will leave her alone."

Delia caught Cynthia's eye and silently applauded her. The Snow Queen dropped her eyes to the floor with embarrassment. It was so sad, thought Delia. She could not take pleasure in finally nailing the lift.

"Better, Cynthia," said Madame in a voice without praise or feeling. "But you vill not dance opening night. You vill perform Christmas Eve. Until then, fast! Drink only vater and juice."

Seconds later, Madame flashed the conductor a festive smile and announced that the Elanova Ballet was ready to begin dress rehearsal. Madame and Miss Dairy took seats in the middle of the theater. The stage emptied, the curtain closed, and the conductor led the orchestra in the overture to the *Nutcracker Suite*. Delia turned to say something, she didn't know what, to Meia Noite, but he had left. She went downstairs to the dressing room, relieved slightly but still worried for her Snow Queen.

As planned, Delia and Claire rehearsed backstage with Miss Tupine during the Star music while Allegra performed onstage. Dancing between the wings and the army of stagehands was awkward and frustrating. In tears, Claire told Miss Tupine that it wasn't fair that she and Delia didn't get to dance on stage. She complained that she didn't feel ready to perform, and Delia echoed her worries. In a surprising show of sympathy, Miss Tupine offered to rehearse each one of them while the musicians took a little break. She ordered the other dancers to clear the stage and rehearsed each of the girls separately for a few minutes. Dancing onstage in costume to

Miss Tupine's counting was calming. Delia executed her double pirouettes easily and felt sure and steady in her Gamba pointe shoes. They were perfectly worn in. Back in her dressing room, she lovingly wrapped the ribbons around the heel and slipped them into her bag.

It was well past ten, the official time given for rehearsal to end, when Madame called the entire cast to the stage. She ordered everyone to take a hot bath before going to bed and to eat a good breakfast but a light lunch the next day. She blessed them in Russian. The company dispersed in high spirits.

Delia looked for her father in the crowd of parents waiting in the lobby. He wasn't there. She went outside and scanned the parking lot. Finally, she saw his car.

But it wasn't her father. It was Pearl.

"Surprise, Little Moon." Pearl hopped out of the car and hugged her, swinging her around in the night.

"What are you doing here?" Delia laughed. "I thought you weren't coming home until Tuesday." Then her face suddenly clouded with worry. "You didn't get expelled, did you?"

"No. Not yet anyway. I had Dad tell you Tuesday so I could surprise you."

The two sisters looked at each other. Dancers and their mothers milled past, hurrying home to observe Madame's orders. Pearl ran a finger across Delia's cheek, wiping off a bit of the stage makeup she had yet to wash off. "You trying to imitate me, Little Moon?"

"You think I want to kill Dad?"

"Yeah, that probably would put him over the edge." Pearl hooked a greasy lock of hair behind her ear. Delia noticed the back of her hands. They were covered with dark drawings of spirals and crescents, asterisks and crosses embedded in a web.

"Are those tattoos?"

"No, it's sugar and henna, you know, that dye you put in your hair. It will last about a month." She spread her fingers for Delia to see. "It's called *mehandi*. Women in Morocco do this for each other. It signifies some sort of change, some important event in your life."

Delia followed one line with her finger in its path across Pearl's hand. "Has there been an important event in your life recently?"

"Maybe. I'm not sure yet. I can't really talk about it. I don't want to jinx it."

"Is it a spell?"

Pearl narrowed her eyes. "Hades let me brush his mane the other day."

It was such a little thing, thought Delia, nothing compared to what she had been working toward.

"Congratulations," she said, trying to sound supportive.

As they passed under a streetlight, Delia caught a glimpse of Pearl's painted hands on the wheel. She thought back to another time when her sister had painted her hands, a Christmas long ago, when Delia still pretended

Pearl was her mother. The sisters sat by the bay window, watching the snow fall and breaking open the pomegranates they found in their stockings. Only Pearl could eat the seeds. They were too bitter for Delia. Pearl broke a seed with her teeth and painted their hands with the red juice.

"Our bones are turning into garnets." She laughed. In those days, she and Pearl were princesses together in their own fairy tale. Then the briars came, the thorns and the spells, and Pearl became lost behind a door without a key.

11

Charms

On Christmas Eve, the day she first danced Star in the two-week run of performances, Delia soaked in a hot tub with witch hazel and herbs. She wore leg warmers all day and ate a light lunch while Pearl massaged her feet and circled her with a wand of burning sage for good luck. She checked and double-checked her ballet bag, packed a sewing kit, and hid one of the feathers Pearl gave her in her bun. Pearl dropped her off at the theater an hour early so that Delia could give herself a complete barre.

A few other dancers were already there. The guest artist, a resplendent Sugar Plum

Fairy who studied with Madame for ten years before she left to dance in a German company, played the grand piano in the orchestra pit. The humiliated Cynthia and her cavalier were on stage in street clothes marking their lifts. The evening's Clara, her hair in curlers, performed pliés at the portable barre in the wings. The stage technicians were watching a football game on a small television. Delia slipped on her sweatpants and began to stretch downstage. She circled her ankles and twisted her spine. She lay on her stomach in straddle splits and melted into the floor.

Her father would be there tonight, and Pearl, and Mr. McGrath with his family. Her father and sister had not seen her dance in years. She never allowed either of them to watch class, and neither had seen the last silly recital she had danced with Miss Sherrie's school. Pearl had been in some sort of crisis, and her father had had to attend to it. Delia had been a tulip in a piece entitled, "Dance of the Little Flowers." She wore a green leotard, green tights, green ballet shoes, and a little green cap with a handful of plastic tulips glued to the top. At the time she was crushed that no one in her family was there to watch, but now she was relieved. Delia lamented the years she wasted at Miss Sherrie's World of Dance with its cramped studios, crass recitals, recorded music, and inferior teachers. Fortunately, she was on the right path now. If she continued to concentrate in class, she told herself, incorporating everything Madame Elanova had to offer, she would dance professionally.

Once she was warmed up, Delia went to her dressing room and began to apply her makeup. The other young soloists of act one, scene one shared the room with her. The military dolls sang the score of *My Fair Lady*, and the dancing doll and Clara, her hair now in long curls, played a game of jacks on the floor. Delia sponged on the pale base makeup and blended it into her neck. She smoothed on eye shadow, soaked a tiny brush in a bead of water, swirled it in a cake of eyeliner, and outlined her eyes. She applied lipstick and blush and put on the false eyelashes. She looked at her painted face in the mirror and was proud. It was the face the two older girls taught her to create, the face Madame wanted to see on all her girls.

Backstage, during the overture, Delia gave herself a little barre. The sequins on her costume glittered as she performed a few ronds de jambe en l'air. Her pointy headpiece made her feel long and tall and confident. Meia Noite was there, stretching a leg on the barre and reaching toward his foot in a long arch. He was supple and strong, both masculine and feminine. Delia stared at his wrists. If they were any more narrow he could be a woman, she thought. She wanted to stop her own stretching and watch him.

"I thought the little blond girl was dancing Star tonight," he said. He wore a huge Brazilian soccer shirt over black leggings. He looked like a skinny little boy. Delia thought she heard disappointment in his voice, and her feelings were hurt.

"No," she replied. "I'm dancing." She injected her response with a touch of defiance.

"Thank God," he answered back. "That blond girl is boring, boring, boring. Like a gymnast she dances! All technique, no life. Who cares for a dancer like this? I'm glad you dance tonight. You have perfect style and expression for this dance. *Merde!*"

He had given her the dancer's blessing for a good performance—a French swear word, and Delia felt as if she had just been initiated. It was bad luck to tell a dancer to break a leg.

At the end of the overture, the curtain lifted, and the stage was flooded with light. Delia waited in the wings not far from Madame. She watched the performance with a wistful expression on her face, her hand at her throat. She hummed the music as she watched Clara dance in the children's waltz.

The appearance of the first mouse just before the clock strikes twelve was Delia's cue to take her place behind the Christmas tree. She crept low to avoid being seen by the audience. She was conscious of Miss Tupine's orders to keep her headpiece well clear of the motorized pulley that enabled the tree to perform its magic of growing up to the ceiling. Years ago, the headpiece of an unlucky Star got stuck in the chain of the pulley. Not only did the tree not grow, but the girl could not free herself and completely missed her solo. Clara was left wandering the stage with her candle, unable to improvise to some of the most dramatic music in the entire *Nutcracker Suite.*

That night, however, things went smoothly. The soldiers and mice created the perfect diversion so that when Delia made her entrance, perfectly timed to the clash of cymbals, it was a surprise to the audience. Her piqué arabesque felt steady and sure, and her chainé turns and pirouettes were fast and sharp. As she beckoned to Clara to trust what lay ahead, she truly believed she was leading her to the Land of the Snow. She was aware of her costume glittering under the lights, but only dimly aware of the orchestra below and the audience beyond. She exited with a grand jeté into the upstage wings, brushing past Madame Elanova, who beamed at her.

Delia stayed backstage in costume for scene three—The Land of the Snow, to see how her beleaguered Snow Queen would fare. Madame watched, too. She cleared her throat and grumbled in Russian when Cynthia wobbled in one of her balances. But she nodded when the lifts went well, and even gave the poor girl a brief hug once the curtain fell on the final tableau.

It was intermission, but before she could walk downstairs to her dressing room, Delia felt a tap on her back. It was Pearl. She had sneaked backstage to bring Delia a bouquet of roses. She wore one of her tattered dresses and a little black hat with a veil. The designs on the back of her hands made it look like she was wearing crocheted gloves.

"Little Moon! Little Moon! My beautiful little sister!" She laughed. "You've gotten so good! You're a little ballerina now!" She gave the roses to Delia and hugged her.

"I hid the feathers you gave me in my hair."

"I could tell!"

From the corner of her eye Delia noticed Madame Elanova hovering by, smiling and waiting to say something.

"Beautiful dancing, my sylph. You could feel it, no?" She kissed Delia on the top of her head, then looked at Pearl and blinked. "And who is this? This is friend?"

"No, Madame." She glanced at Pearl, taking in the white face makeup, the eyeliner and red lips, the oily hair and the painted hands. In a moment she saw her as Madame did, and she felt embarrassed to introduce her. "This is my sister, Pearl . . . she used to take ballet."

"Indeed," Madame replied.

"I didn't like it," said Pearl with a laugh. "It was too controlling for me."

"Yes, ballet is not for you. But your sister is different."

Delia hoped that Pearl had missed the disparagement in Madame's demeanor, but Pearl had not missed a thing.

With that, Madame turned away. She touched the scarf at her neck with an elegant display of hand, then sailed to the Snow Queen, caressing her with a voice full of affection and approval.

"Nice, Cynthia, very nice. Just a few more pounds to lose my dear, just a bit more around the hips, and then you vill be lovely. Everything vill be better—the lifts, the balances, the line of the leg . . ."

The relief on Cynthia's face disintegrated. She looked as wounded and afraid as she did at dress rehearsal. Pearl watched in fascination.

"Why is she hassling that girl?" she asked. "She's beautiful. She danced like a goddess."

"That's the way Madame is. She's always encouraging us to be better."

Pearl shook her head. "She doesn't seem very encouraging to me. I'm making you an amulet. That woman is dangerous." And then Pearl flicked her hands in the air as if she were shaking off an evil spirit.

12

Gifts

Mr. Ferri took a tiny bite of pastry and sneered. It was the first time he had eaten anything with more than a gram of fat in months. "Are these any good?" he asked. "They're from the Georgetown store. I don't trust that baker Flavio hired."

It was Christmas morning and Mr. Ferri and his daughters were in the living room, having coffee and pastries and opening presents.

Delia took a tiny bite and forced herself to swallow. It could not, she assured herself, have more than thirty calories. "They're fine, Daddy," she replied.

"It's dry," shouted Mr. Ferri.

"I haven't been able to eat those things in years," said Pearl. "Even when they're fresh they totally gross me out." She dunked a powdered doughnut in her coffee and took a relishing bite. "Where's my next present?"

Mr. Ferri handed her a red box with an enormous gold bow. Pearl tore into it. It was a black velvet riding hat.

"The headmistress tells me you've been spending most of your free time with your horse," Mr. Ferri said. "She says you're becoming an excellent horsewoman."

"I don't know if I'd say excellent," said Pearl. "I like being around Hades. He's by far the most interesting person at that school." She put on the hat and went to look at herself in the mirror in the dining room. "Hey, I like this hat!"

"It's a real English riding hat," Mr. Ferri went on. "It meets all the requirements if you want to compete in horse shows."

"I don't think there's much chance of that." She continued to admire herself in the mirror. "I think I'll make an entire riding outfit in stretchy black lace."

"An interest in horses, competition in shows look very good on your application to college," he added. "It's time to start thinking about that."

"College? I'm not going to college. I'm barely making it through high school, and this is the easiest school I've been to yet. You just save all your money for Little Moon. She's the one who's going to college."

"No, I'm not," said Delia. "I'm going to New York to dance."

"Great idea!" said Pearl.

"My daughters are going to college!" shouted Mr. Ferri. "Do you know how much I wanted to go to college? But I was never given the choice. I had a family business to run."

Mr. Ferri stormed into the kitchen and made himself another cappuccino. Delia and

Pearl exchanged glances and sighed.

"Poor Dad," said Pearl. "First I was such a disappointment, and now you . . ."

"I shouldn't have said anything about New York," said Delia, shaking her head.

"Don't worry about it, Little Moon. He'll forget you ever said it. In his mind, you're going to college, and that's that."

When their father returned, the family settled back down into its Christmas routine. From her father Delia received ballet books, including one with a photo of a very young Alicia Elanova, and a gift certificate for her favorite record store.

Delia gave Pearl and her father the books she had picked out for them. For her father she chose a history of the Tour de France; for Pearl, a collection of prayers and songs from native cultures around the world.

Finally, Pearl distributed her presents. She gave her father something she called a "kind of kaleidoscope." It was a long, narrow

glass jar filled with flour and little artifacts—
butterfly wings and quartz, marbles and
shells, fragments of honeycomb, the fuzzy
body of a bee. Mr. Ferri turned it slowly and
watched the flour shift and bury, hide and
reveal the tiny treasures. He was silent for
some time, unable to say thank you or to
remark on the present he had received.
"This is very nice," he finally said. "Thank
you, Pearl."

"Close your eyes," Pearl commanded
Delia. "I didn't have time to wrap this." She
dropped a small blue pillow into Delia's hands.
An embroidered image of a female figure
stood with her arms outstretched. Blue, purple, and green birds flew around her. The pillow smelled of lavender and mint. Delia held it
to the side of her face as if she were sleeping,
smiling with her eyes closed.

"It's stuffed with goose down and special
herbs for your dancing. I ripped open my com-
forter at school to make it."

"Who is she?" Delia touched the tiny stitches.

"I don't know. Some goddess. Sleep with her. Your dreams will tell you her name."

Pearl set down her coffee and ran off to her bedroom. She came back a moment later with two small packages. "I have one more present for each of you," she announced. "Here." She handed Delia and her father a package each. It was a framed picture of some sort. They opened them. They were the old photos of Mrs. Ferri. Delia's heart began to beat hard and fast.

"Where . . . where did you get this?" Mr. Ferri asked. In his hands he held the picture of his wife in her bridal dress.

"I found them in your office. You had taken them down and forgotten about them." Pearl's eyes glistened and her voice trembled slightly. "We can't keep pretending Mom never existed. We're all so sad, and so is she. Her spirit is aching because none of us talk about her."

Delia could not speak. She stared at the photo of her mother, smiling in her baker's outfit, then turned it facedown in her lap. She was afraid her father might break into tears, or throw the photo across the room and yell at Pearl to mind her own business and not go through his things.

Mr. Ferri dropped his face in his hand. He was quiet for a long time. Finally he spoke.

"Thank you, Pearl. Merry Christmas, daughters." And then he left to go ride his bike.

"It was too much for him," said Pearl. "Too strong a dose."

"You think that was medicine?" asked Delia.

"I think it's reality. He had a wife. He had two daughters with her. She died. He's sad. You and I are sad. He can't just keep trying to ignore everything."

Delia felt a rush of love for her father, and she wanted to protect him from Pearl's judgment. "Maybe he's not sad," she said. "And maybe he doesn't miss Mom. I'm not sad about Mom dying. Honestly, I hardly ever think of her. Only when you're around. I think what you did was selfish. You're trying to force Dad and me to feel exactly like you do."

"Don't you get it, Little Moon? I'm trying to force you two to *feel*. Both of you have locked up your feelings—Dad with all that fitness nonsense and you with ballet—because you can't deal with Mom's death."

"You're the one who can't deal with Mom's death. Dad and I are just fine. You can't even handle getting to school on time or passing a stupid class like Math Fundamentals—that's why Dad had to send you away to that school."

Pearl looked at her sister calmly and walked out, and Delia was alone in the living room surrounded by torn paper and empty boxes. She picked up the pillow Pearl had made for her and traced the image of the woman calling the birds. How could Pearl say she did not feel? She knew nothing about her really, nothing about what she felt when she heard music or when she danced. Her father understood her better. He proved it in the presents he gave her. She had heard Madame once say that a dancer's life was lonely. *It was true*, thought Delia, *and if Pearl and I are going to grow further and further apart, so be it.*

13

Swans

The holidays came and went. Pearl had another week of lounging about the house before classes at the Highton School resumed. She spent hours in her room, talking to her old pals Summer and Locke on the phone, reading esoteric books on the tarot and meditation, and casting spells. Delia and Claire returned to their lackluster classes at Markham Middle School with a case of post-*Nutcracker* depression. Nothing there could match the excitement of putting on stage makeup, taking a barre in costume, or dancing in the spotlight before hundreds of people. The only thing they had to look forward to was the afternoon tea Madame Elanova held every January for a select few of her students.

It was a secret event that everyone at the studio knew about. This year, as every year, several girls were bitterly disappointed that they were not invited. Tears were shed and mothers swore to turn their daughters over to another ballet teacher. Few did.

Pearl drove Delia to the event. "I should be wearing a chauffeur's outfit," she said when she saw her sister in her best dress, stockings and heels. "Is this some sort of royal audience?"

"Sort of," giggled Delia. "It's only for Madame's favorite dancers. She calls us her sylphs."

"Wow," said Pearl, shaking her head in disbelief. "And I guess all of you like being called that."

"It's an honor," said Delia.

Tea was held in the living room of Madame's apartment. Delia sat on the divan like the other girls, her back straight, ankles crossed. All the sylphs were there, dressed as if they were attending a matinee performance at the Kennedy Center. They raised cups of tea to their lips, nibbled Russian teacakes, and giggled behind cupped hands. Only Cynthia did not eat or drink. She stood off to one side gazing at a portrait of Madame in the title role of *Giselle*.

Delia, Claire, and Allegra drifted through the apartment together, regarding Madame's mementos. There was much to look at. A baby grand piano covered with stacks of music filled one corner of the room. Above it was a photograph of Madame and other members of Les Ballets Russes on a steamer bound for London. A glass case enclosing the rotting pointe shoes of Anna Pavlova adorned one side table, and a bust of Madame by the great Belair graced the other. In a shadow box, illuminated by its own overhead light, were the sketches Nijinsky made while choreographing *L'Après-Midi d'un*

Faun. Madame's mentor, the ballerina Olga Korsovina, had danced in the premier performance at the Paris Opera. She had passed the drawings and Pavlova's slippers on to Madame shortly before her death. Delia listened as Madame spoke of visiting her teacher's deathbed. Next to her stood the two anorexics with their hands clasped as if they were praying.

"Vords cannot express my sadness on that day. Korsovina vas my mother, my teacher, my inspiration—all these things and more! There she vas. Pale and veak, thin as skeleton, hours avay from death. She took my hand and said, 'Alicia, you must promise to pass on our legacy. Promise me that vone day you vill open a school so that the tradition of our teachers continues.' I opened my heart, my soul and promised I vould do so. And that is vat I have done. I have dedicated my life to teaching in the great tradition of the Russian ballet."

The drama of the dying mentor and the

youthful Madame swearing her devotion filled Delia with strange longing. Madame's story told of something that might have been lost forever. The chain that linked Delia to a tradition that crossed continents and generations could have been broken. And then she would have been what she once was—a motherless girl with a busy father and an unhappy sister, a girl who did her homework and danced in recitals. But because of Madame, Delia belonged to something old and grand, something fragile, beautiful, but vivid. She could see it in the way she and the other sylphs opened their arms in port de bras. It was the language their bodies spoke.

"And now," said Madame with good cheer, "I have important announcement for all my sylphs. Please, sit down. Listen to all I have to say to you." Like a flock of birds the girls returned to their places simultaneously. Madame sat in a gilt chair and folded her hands. She cleared her throat. "Vhen I am surrounded by my sylphs as I am now, I think of everything I vant to pass on to my sylphs."

"Tell us about the swans," encouraged one of the older girls.

"Oh, the stories I could tell you! The bickering svans! Did you know that svans bicker? They are not sveet creatures, oh no, they are not." She laughed again and looked amazingly young. "Still Korsovina kept them at her home in London. 'Vatch them!' she commanded. I vas only sixteen. I had just entered the company. She vas dissatisfied vith my arms in *Svan Lake*. 'Spend a veek vith me and study my svans,' she insisted. So I did. And I learned."

"Tell us about the archduke and the ruby," said Claire. She knew the story from her mother.

"Ah, the archduke . . ." Madame waved him away. "Neither are vorth discussing at the moment. Some day I vill tell you, but not today. Today ve talk of ballet. Ve talk of ballet and my most precious dream, my dream for my own company. I look around me now and I see beautiful girls, beautiful girls vith talent and love for ballet, and I say to myself, 'Now is time for your dream to come true.'"

And then Madame went on to describe her plans, how she had received funding from an anonymous benefactor, a commitment from the theater to host a spring performance, and how a former star of the Ballet Metropolitan in New York had agreed to stage the masterpiece *Adagio Classique* with the fledgling company.

"This is very beautiful, very important vork. My favorite ballet by Prokov," she explained in a hushed voice. "It is perfect for you, Alexis, vith your legs, for you, Elizabeth, vith your pirouettes, and for all of my sylphs vith your Russian épaulement. *Adagio Classique* demands a very disciplined corps de ballet. All of you must vork hard, very, very hard! But this you already know, and that is vhy you are my sylphs."

The company of sylphs responded to the announcement as solemnly as if they were present at a ritual. Delia felt a swell of excitement. It cast her about in images of rehearsals and performances. There would be long afternoons in the studio, music to memorize, and steps to learn. How wonderful it felt to be away from home, to be in a place where people saw her and appreciated her for who she was— a dancer, a person who wanted a life of dance and beauty, music and art.

The following Monday, Delia returned to Markham Middle School with a delicious sense of being above it all. The juvenile theatrics of her fellow seventh-graders seemed more silly and banal than ever. She went to her classes, ate lunch with Claire, completed worksheets, took notes, and copied down her assignments.

The only part of the school day she looked forward to was history with Mr. McGrath. Lately, he had been lecturing on the westward expansion and its devastating impact upon the lives of the Plains Indians. He described the debilitating effects of life on the reservation and the numerous treaties the U.S. government made and broke because of the rampant greed and recklessness of the American people. Even though she could make no connection to her passion for ballet and its history, Delia was fascinated. It bothered her somewhat. She wondered what to do with this curiosity for something Madame would find completely insignificant.

The bell rang. Delia swept her notebook and pen into her backpack and headed for the door.

"Wait, wait, wait, little dancer," said Mr. McGrath. "I have something to say to you. You were fantastic! You were wonderful! My little girl dances around the house saying, 'I'm Delia! I'm Delia!'"

"Thank you." She blushed.

"No, really, my wife and I were very impressed. And my daughter thinks you're a princess, a real princess. She actually asked me if you were a princess."

Delia laughed. "Maybe she'd like a pair of my old pointe shoes. She could hang them on the wall."

"Would she like that? Are you kidding? She'll probably sleep with them under her pillow."

"I have another performance coming up in the spring. Maybe you'll bring her to that."

"Count on it. We're all members of the Delia Ferri fan club."

Later that day, Madame taught an especially difficult pointe class. She was, Delia and every other sylph knew, figuring out who would be given what part in *Adagio Classique* and stirring up the competition as Claire had once said. Delia had seen the ballet performed once when the Ballet Metropolitan was in town, but she was most familiar with it from photographs in her ballet books. The cast included three soloists, a lead couple, plus a large corps that divided into smaller groups then rejoined throughout the ballet. There was a well-known section, famous from innumerable photographs, where the entire company nearly ran across the stage one by one in a series of piqué arabesques. The speed of the simple step demanded tremendous strength and balance. To test the ability of her girls, Madame had them perform the step from one corner of the studio to the other over and over. After her third time across the floor, Delia could feel a blister develop on her toe. She peeled back her tights to look at it. Already a layer of skin had separated and filled with water. She was rummaging through her bag for her bandages when she heard a sound like ripping cloth, a short, surprised cry, and a thud.

It was Allegra. For a few bars, the other girls went on dancing and Mr. Guest went on playing. But Allegra did not move. Her face was red, and she seemed to be short of breath. She took in great gulps of air through her mouth. Finally, Madame rose from the bench, and the music and the dancing stopped. Allegra tried to get up but fell back to the floor like a broken toy.

"It's her knee," whispered one of the girls.

"It's her ankle," whispered another.

"Someone," called out Madame in a calm, firm voice, "get ice from the office."

Immediately, Cynthia ran downstairs to the office. The sylph who would take over the studio one day sprang into action. She bent down to help Allegra up and walked her slowly to the bench. Two blotches of red bloomed on Allegra's cheeks, and she winced with each little hop to the front of the studio.

"Prop up the leg," said Madame. The older sylph pulled up a chair, put a ballet bag on it, and gently placed Allegra's wounded leg on top. Madame watched with a slight frown. *She's angry at her*, realized Delia. *She's mad at Allegra for getting hurt.*

Girls hung back in the corners of the studio as if they had witnessed a car accident. A few minutes later, Cynthia returned with ice packs for her knee and told Madame that Allegra's guardian was on her way.

"Very good," said Madame. "Girls, let's continue. Mr. Guest, please . . ."

During révérence, the couple Allegra lived with carried her out of the studio. Her arms were looped around their shoulders, and they made a little seat for her with their forearms. Delia couldn't help but watch them make their way out of the studio. She wondered who would call Allegra's mother in Florida, and she remembered the story of Maya, the sylph who was so injured in a fall that she had to give up dancing. A dark question rooted inside her. *Is Allegra seriously hurt? Will this be enough to keep her out of* Adagio Classique?

Girls retreated to the dressing rooms and immediately began to revisit the event and dissect Allegra's fall. The various jealousies and tensions among the sylphs dissipated, and for a few moments they bonded over discussion of the nature of the injury. One girl said she saw Allegra's knee twist when she fell. Another said she saw her fall directly on her kneecap. The anorexics did not participate in the discussion. Occasionally, Delia saw them catch each other's dark eyes. They left without a word.

"Did you hear the ripping sound?" asked one girl.

"What was that?" asked Delia. "It made me sick to my stomach."

"I bet it was a tendon," answered Claire.

"I bet she won't be in *Adagio Classique*," said another.

"Not if she tore a tendon," agreed Cynthia sadly.

No, thought Delia, *not if she tore a tendon*. Instantly, Delia felt a sharp pang of hope. If Allegra was out for several weeks, she would have a good chance of being cast in *Adagio Classique*. If Allegra were out for longer, months even, perhaps Madame would forget her and turn more of her attention on Delia. *I can be mean,* Delia thought. *Ballet is making me mean.*

At home she was restless and uncomfortable. She could feel herself turning into someone she didn't know, someone who was competitive and unfeeling. It was late when she knocked on Pearl's door.

"Could I have caused it?" she asked. The sisters sat on the floor facing each other. "I want a part in *Adagio Classique* so badly, and she has a much better chance of getting it than I do. I don't remember wishing she would fall, but I have wished she would just go away so that I could get the part."

"No," said Pearl. "You didn't cause it. Only a very powerful witch who practices black magic can curse someone like that," said Pearl. "The witch doesn't actually make her fall. It's much more subtle than that. Instead, she causes the person to doubt herself. The curse is the lack of faith she causes within the victim. It takes time. It is deliberate and callous. You don't have it in you, Little Moon. Neither do I. I only practice white magic."

"I wonder if anyone cursed Allegra."

"It's possible," said Pearl. "From what I hear about the ballet world there might be a few people practicing black magic at your school, including Madame herself. Frankly, I thought she was cursing me the night I met her backstage after you danced Star."

"Oh, Pearl," scoffed Delia. "That's ridiculous! Why would Madame curse you?"

"Because I see her. I saw how she destroyed that poor Snow Queen with just a few words about her weight. That girl felt beautiful, and Madame made her feel ugly. And I see how she uses all of you to make her believe she's still a prima ballerina. I'm sure she's capable of cursing anyone who stands up to her, or reminds her she's just a faded old dancer."

"No," said Delia, shaking her head. "Madame's harsh sometimes, but she's training us to become dancers. She's not cursing any of us."

"I bet if you think about it, you could name a couple of girls Madame is cursing, not training. I mean cursing—causing girls to feel badly about themselves, to hate their bodies, to feel ugly and inferior . . ."

Delia shrugged impatiently. Pearl and her witchcraft were so ridiculous. She thought it gave her knowledge into everything, but it did not. She didn't understand ballet. You had to sacrifice to learn its technique, and this included accepting Madame's tirades, her insults and glares. "Madame is completely devoted to passing on everything she knows to us. She loves us."

"She doesn't love any of you! Not really. She's obsessed with the ones who look like she did when she was young. I bet she even sees her face on their bodies when they dance. They help her pretend she's still a prima ballerina. She's obsessed with the ones she can show off to the big companies in New York or Europe, so everyone will admire her and remember how great she once was. She ignores the rest of her students."

"Madame gives her attention to everyone, not just the ones who are going to dance professionally."

"Oh, please. Name one girl she loves, *loves*, who doesn't have a perfect ballet body but is a good dancer."

Delia fumbled for a name. There was the older sylph who would return after college to teach at the Elanova School. She did not have an ideal body for ballet, and Madame respected her. But it was true; she did not love her the way she did some of her other sylphs. She thought of some of the older girls, who danced with humor and life, whose legs and feet were strong, but not perfectly shaped. They were true dancers, but Madame did not love them. "It's not Madame's fault," she said angrily. "That's the way ballet is."

"So why do you want it so badly, Little Moon?"

"Because it's beautiful!" Delia's eyes filled with tears.

Pearl was sorry she pressed her point so hard. "All I'm really trying to say, Little Moon, is that you have to be careful with Madame. Don't work so hard to please her. I have a feeling she's the type of person you can never really please. Let's light some incense for Allegra. You'll feel better if you wish her well."

Pearl rummaged through her bag. She pulled out a thick braid of dried grass. "This is sweet grass," she said as she lit it. A thin line of blue smoke curled and scented the air. "It's very healing," Pearl said. "Close your eyes and imagine this smoke traveling to Allegra." Delia followed her sister's directions. For a few moments, she forgot about her striving for the role and the competition Madame had orchestrated between Allegra,

Claire, and herself. She breathed in the sweet smoke and thought of Allegra sitting at home with her knee bandaged and healing, and for a moment she was able to wish her a swift recovery. And Pearl was right; it felt good.

14

Adagio

"Well, Little Moon, I'm off, bound for the desolation of the Highton School." It was Sunday morning and Pearl was taking the train back to school. The sisters stood in the doorway of Delia's room, Delia still in pajamas, Pearl in black. She had dyed her hair black and was wearing her geisha face and skull necklace for the occasion.

"Are you sad?" asked Delia.

"Not really. I'm glad to be getting back to Hades. I'm doing some good work there, not schoolwork, witch work. It's quiet, and the woods are beautiful."

"How long is the train ride?"

"Three hours. I'm bringing the book of prayers you gave me. It's right here." She patted her bag.

Delia walked her sister to the car, shivering in the gray morning. Mr. Ferri put Pearl's suitcase in the trunk. He reached out to wipe away some of Pearl's makeup. Pearl raised her hand to protect herself.

"Stop it," she said, "Let's go. I don't want to miss my train. Oh, Little Moon, I left you something on your bed!"

Delia stood on the driveway waving good-bye until the car was out of sight. She thought of the ordeal with the photographs and her analysis of Madame. She was glad Pearl was gone. Rehearsals for *Adagio Classique* were scheduled to begin soon, and she needed to concentrate.

On her bed, in the middle of her pillow, she found a sky-blue envelope. Something round and puffy about the size of a hazelnut was inside. Delia held it in her hand. It had the weight of a few coins and smelled like dirt. *It's the amulet*, she thought. *How creepy*. She didn't open the envelope. Instead she tossed it in her desk drawer.

The phone rang. It was Claire.

"Have you heard? Allegra tore a ligament in her knee. She's on crutches."

"How long will she be out?" asked Delia.

"Depends on what the orthopedic surgeon says. She's going to New York next week to see a famous dance surgeon who operates on all the Ballet Metropolitan dancers. She'll be at rehearsal Thursday night, watching. She doesn't want to miss that."

"Of course not," Delia replied. Not only was the Elanova School in its usual state of pre-cast list jitters, it was also anticipating the arrival of the great retired ballerina Christine Dorain, who was to stage *Adagio Classique* with the young company. Miss Dorain began her lessons at the school of the Ballet Metropolitan as a child, joined the company at sixteen, and danced for Mr. Prokov until an injured hip forced her to retire. Although she was never his muse, she was his dependable second fiddle. After his death, because of her devotion to him and her photographic memory of every single step in every ballet he ever choreographed, she came to be considered the living link to Prokov. She traveled the world leading workshops and staging his ballets. Her legacy and position in the dance world filled the sylphs with awe, and all were eager for her arrival.

Days passed uneventfully. Finally it was Thursday, the day of the first rehearsal with Miss Dorain. She entered the studio during the last half of the four o'clock ballet class. Long and lanky, she was a full head taller than Madame. She wore crystal earrings, tie-dyed dance pants, and an enormous sweatshirt that said

Christine Dorain
Official Psychic for Mr. P.

If it were not for her graying hair and the wrinkles on her forehead, Miss Dorain could have been in her twenties. Madame beckoned her to sit beside her on the bench. Allegra moved her crutches aside to make room for her. Miss Dorain and Madame watched the girls fly across the floor in the grand waltz combination. They pointed to different girls and whispered. Delia and Claire guessed they were deciding the cast.

"Poor Allegra," said Delia. "She must be so frustrated."

Claire shrugged. "There will be other ballets for Allegra," she replied.

Class ended and Madame Elanova reminded the girls they had only a short break before rehearsal at six fifteen. Delia, Claire and the others went downstairs to rest their feet. The anorexics plugged in their electric teakettle to make instant coffee. Other girls munched on carrots and rice cakes. A few girls tried to cram in a half hour of homework. Delia and

Claire visited the vending machine for a diet soda.

Girls began to wander back to the studio. They rested a leg on the barre, or sat in straddle splits, hands on knees. Miss Dorain was blasting the score and hooking up a tiny TV to a video player so the girls could see a tape of the most recent Ballet Metropolitan production of *Adagio Classique*. She scurried about with cords and equipment while simultaneously carrying on an animated conversation with Madame.

Delia and Claire stretched with the others, waiting for Miss Dorain to begin. A few of the girls speculated that Madame commissioned *Adagio Classique* especially to convince the destined sylph to stay with the company instead of going off to New York. After all, they reasoned, if Madame is truly to have a company, she needs to keep her best dancers, and the only way to do that is to give them the chance to dance great choreography.

"Why not stay here and dance leading roles in works like this instead of slaving in the corps of some New York company?" asked one girl.

"Because New York is still New York," said another.

"But every New York company had a beginning. Maybe the Elanova Ballet will be a big success."

"No way. No one is starting companies anymore. Except Madame and she's crazy." Delia stared at the girl who said this, a strong technician who was only sixteen. She was splayed in the splits, her chest and chin on the floor. She sounded so sure of herself, and Delia wondered if she was right.

Rehearsal began without introduction or inspiring speech. Miss Dorain began at the beginning.

"Okay, let's learn the opening. I need you, you, you, you, and you. You five are the back row. Just stand there in the order I called you.

Don't do anything yet. Okay. Next row. Let's see you, you, and you. Alicia, refresh my memory, who is my lead? Who are my soloists? Is it these two? Where are the three small girls for the front line?"

The casting was predictable. Once again, the abused Cynthia had dieted herself thin and was cast as one of the two soloists. The college-bound sylph was the other. The destined sylph was the lead. The three girls in the front row were the two anorexics and either Delia, Claire, or Allegra. Madame called the three candidates over to the piano. Allegra stood up with the help of her crutches to listen.

"If Allegra cannot dance in performance, Delia or Claire vill have the part," said Madame. "All three of you must listen to Miss Dorain as if the part vas yours and no vone else's. No vone knows vhat might happen. Maybe, Allegra's knee heals in time, maybe not. Maybe Miss Dorain and I decide part goes to Delia, maybe ve give it to Claire. No vone knows, only God. So all of you must pay attention and concentrate. Listen, vatch, and practice. Yes? Good girls. Delia, you dance first half of rehearsal, and Claire, you dance second."

The three girls nodded in unison with polite expressions on their faces. Delia took her place in the front line between the two anorexics. Claire went to the back of the studio to learn the steps. The wounded Allegra watched mournfully from the bench, marking the steps with her hands.

Miss Dorain taught the girls the steps to the first movement of the piece. It involved the entire corps, which formed and re-formed elaborate patterns several times. Few of the steps were difficult, but the speed at which they were to be performed was extremely challenging. Miss Dorain's corrections were brutally honest.

"You two!" She pointed at the anorexics. "You both made boo-boos. Enormous boo-boos on a nothing step!" At another she yelled, "You stupid girl, this is Tchaikovsky, not Stravinsky." To some girls sitting on the floor while she was rehearsing one of the soloists' parts she said, "Don't ever just sit on the floor or hang on the barre in rehearsal. You might not be the first one chosen, but you might be the one who can do the step. So stand up and practice every part. That's how I got the lead in *Concertina*. At first Mr. P. gave it to some-one else, someone I did *not* like very much, but I learned the part, and practiced it in the back of the studio whenever she danced. I did it on purpose to freak her out, and guess what hap-pened? *I* danced it at the premiere!"

Delia was silent, alert, and focused. She did her best to ignore Claire at the back of the stu-dio learning her steps along with her. *I want this*, she thought to herself. Star had been given to her. She didn't know enough back then to work for a part, but this one she wanted. The clock was ticking, and soon it would be time for Claire to take over. But before she did, Delia received a sort of blessing from Miss Dorain that would sustain her even as she struggled with the choreography.

It was the third or fourth time that Miss Dorain rehearsed the very opening, a slow, simple pattern of steps that set the tone for the entire piece. When the curtain opened, the entire corps was still for several bars in an elegant pose. Each dancer stood with her feet parallel, her right arm extended, her gaze over the hand. Frustrated, Miss Dorain stopped the tape again.

"No, no, no! You can't just stand in this pose. You have to yearn in it. You have to aspire! Only Delia has the proper feeling," she announced. "It should feel like you're in heaven, or with God. This is the spirit of *Adagio Classique*. It's a beyond feeling. How old are you? Thirteen? This is young to know this feeling. All of you should watch Delia in this pose."

There, thought Delia, *I'll get the part*. She

didn't have to curse Allegra or wish Claire would make a mistake. She would get the part because of something only she had. It must be the same thing that Madame saw in her that first day. She wished Pearl was home to tell her how wrong she was about Madame. Madame wasn't using her. She saw her for who she really was—a dancer.

15

Amulet

That evening in her room, Delia read Pearl's letter. The amulet was a tiny crocheted bag no bigger than the end of her thumb.

> *This is the amulet I promised you. Inside*
> *are dried flowers and a little mirror*
> *pushed into a bit of beeswax. The mirror*
> *will deflect any bad thoughts Madame*
> *what's-her-face sends your way and bounce*
> *them back to her. I've been saving these*
> *ingredients for myself, but you need them*
> *more than I do. The amulet will help you*
> *keep your own strength and purity when*

Madame tries to make you doubt yourself.
Wear it whenever you're around her, and
stop thinking of her as your mother. I'm
serious—that woman is a bad witch.

Love,
Pearl

No way, thought Delia. *Madame's no bad witch. You're just a confused one.* Pearl had to be kidding. There was absolutely no way she was going to dance with a creepy voodoo bag around her neck. She buried it under some sweaters in drawer of her dresser.

In her bath, Delia thought about Pearl's overreaction to Madame. How ridiculous it was. Of course she didn't think of Madame as her mother. Pearl could never understand. She didn't know what it was like to have a teacher you loved and respected. *How sad*, Delia thought, as she soaked in the warm water. She lifted handfuls of water to her face and washed away the dirt and sweat of rehearsal, feeling as strong and pure as she ever wanted to be.

"What time did you get to bed last night?" thundered Mr. Ferri outside Delia's room. Delia had overslept, and it exasperated him. It threw his whole schedule off, and he would have to cut his morning ride short.

"Eleven." Delia yawned. "I took a bath and did my homework after dinner."

"Why didn't you do your homework during the breaks at rehearsals?"

"They aren't long enough. Miss Dorain has to teach us the entire ballet before she leaves on Monday."

"What is this ballet? I thought there wasn't another performance until *Nutcracker*."

"It's called *Adagio Classique*. It's going to be part of the spring performance, Daddy."

"Since when does Madame have a spring performance?"

"She's forming a company, the Elanova Ballet. We won't just be dancing *Nutcracker* anymore. We'll have spring and summer performances. We might even go on tour."

"Miss Sherrie only had one performance a year."

"Madame is not Miss Sherrie, Dad."

"Well, you listen to me. If you fall behind in your schoolwork, if I see you looking too tired, you're out. You're too young to be working so hard. Your health and education are the most important things."

"Yes, Dad," Delia replied. Her father's threats were as frightening as paper airplanes. She had no doubt that she could do it all. After all, she was the only one with the proper feeling in the opening pose of *Adagio Classique*.

At school the next day, Delia and Claire met at their usual table in the cafeteria. Both of them scratched out a bit of homework as they chatted and ate. They were in rehearsal mode, which meant trying to get as many things done at the same time as possible. They giggled about the New Age elements in Miss Dorain's wardrobe—the tie-dye and crystals, the reference to psychic powers on her sweat-shirt—and reviewed their rehearsal schedule. There would be one tonight, and again on Saturday and Sunday afternoon. Miss Dorain would return to New York, and Madame would run rehearsals until the week before the performance. Then Miss Dorain would return to lead them through the dress rehearsal and watch the performance.

The most pressing topic of conversation was one they would not broach. They never mentioned the role for which they were com-peting against each other, nor did they go over its steps. They shared their thoughts about everything else regarding *Adagio Classique*—how the soloists were doing with their parts, who in the corps kept messing up the lines, which was the most difficult section. But they never talked about who would dance Allegra's part. For surely Allegra was doomed. It had been two weeks since she fell, and she could barely stand. A torn ligament in the knee, whether slight or major, kept a dancer out of the studio for months. Claire had it on good authority. Her mother told her so.

There was something between them now, and it hung about in their shared spaces of school and studio. They no longer stretched together before class or stood next to each other at the barre. Once Delia pretended not to see Claire in the hall at Markham Middle School. She passed her without a word. One evening she let the answering machine pick up a message from Claire and never returned the call. Delia's determination scared her, for she knew she was willing to sacrifice her friendship with Claire to get the part. She thought of her secret satisfaction when Allegra fell. But when she worried that she was not the same person that she used to be, she cast the thought away. It was how a dancer had to be, she told herself.

"My dad must have erased the message," she told her the next day.

The same tense excitement present at Miss Dorain's first rehearsal permeated all the others. She ran the girls through the old steps and taught them new ones. She called them over to see the videotape to study how the lines crossed and folded in different sections of the choreography. The soloists exasperated her with their inability to execute one of the more famous sections of the ballet. One girl takes a piqué arabesque while another girl promenades her around in a circle. Cynthia struck the arabesque but could not keep her balance when the girl promenaded her.

"Here, promenade me," said Miss Dorain. She took a piqué arabesque and Cynthia's partner promenaded her around in a circle. Miss Dorain was flawless. She did not wobble a bit. She turned to Cynthia and said, "If I can do this at my age with an artificial hip so can you. I don't want to shame you into it, but there you are." Cynthia practiced it again but failed to execute the step.

"I want the corps to disappear for twenty minutes," Miss Dorain called out. "I need an empty studio so I can really see what's going on with my soloists. It isn't pretty, I can tell you that!"

"Let's do some homework," said Delia, grateful that she had found something to say to Claire.

"Great idea," she replied.

The two girls diagrammed a few sentences together with relish. The logic of the activity was an excellent antidote to the drama in which they found themselves. It made them giddy. They made up names for the grammatical terms—proposition for preposition, nin for noun, berv for verb—and giggled as they completed the exercise. It was a relief to be out of the studio, away from the judgment of Miss Dorain and Madame, away from the ongoing criticism of poor Cynthia.

"Madame is so mean to her," said Delia.

"Madame always picks on someone."

"But why her? She picked on her in *Nutcracker*, too."

"Because she's right on the borderline of making it professionally," replied Claire. "Her legs and feet are pretty, but she isn't quite strong enough to sail through an audition. And she *has* to keep her weight down."

"But maybe Madame should be more gentle. I bet Cynthia would get stronger and skinnier if Madame weren't so harsh."

"If that's what she needs she should quit ballet. Believe me, no company director or ballet master in New York is any nicer than Madame."

"But she's such a pretty dancer. I hope Madame doesn't drive her to quit."

"I don't think she will," said Claire. "She's getting tougher, which is good. Did you see how she reacted when Miss Dorain got frustrated with her just now? She didn't even flinch."

"She's becoming like the anorexics," Delia said sadly. Fear and loss drifted over her head like twin clouds. Delia shivered. She didn't agree with Claire. How could becoming unfeeling help a dancer? Sooner or later, wouldn't it hurt her dancing? She scribbled a note on her notebook, telling herself to find a way to sneak Pearl's amulet into Cynthia's ballet bag.

At home, later that night, she fished out the amulet from her drawer. She sniffed the dried flowers and felt the tiny cross-stitches Pearl had worked into the fabric. It was strangely heavy for something so small. She closed her palm around it and decided not to give it to Cynthia. *I might need it myself*, she thought.

16

Disguise

Delia was not surprised when Madame told Delia and Claire that Allegra would indeed need an operation and be unable to dance for several months. She pulled the two girls aside at the beginning of Saturday's rehearsal. Small groups of girls dotted the studio, chatting and stretching. Madame held the two girls by the hand.

"You, Claire, vill take her part. Delia, you vill be understudy for the corps. If any other girl is unable to dance, you vill dance her part."

"Thank you, Madame," whispered Claire.

Delia was unable to talk. She forced a

cheerful expression on her face, but the impulse to cry coursed through her. She did not. When Miss Dorain began rehearsal Claire took her place in the front of the line, and Delia went to the back of the studio. She marked the steps with the music, but the heaviness in her heart made it hard to dance.

At the break, Delia avoided the dressing room. She didn't want to see or talk to anyone, least of all Claire. She wandered into the other end of the Elanova School, where the small studios were rented out to other teachers. There was the same eclectic group she remembered from the fall evening long ago. Layers of percussion, shakers, bells, and drums echoed in the hallway. Delia peeked into one of the studios to see Meia Noite teaching a class. He was dancing alone to the drums, demonstrating a step. His eyes were open, and he walked regally with one hand at the back of his head, the other in front of him as if he were looking into a mirror. He walked on the balls of his feet—stepping out to the right then crossing over with his left foot, then going in the opposite direction. Meia signaled to the drummers to stop, then turned to the class. "This dance is prayer to Imenja, *orisha* of love and beauty. *Orisha* is our word for a god or spirit. It is an African word that came to Brazil with the slaves. Imenja is a queen, beautiful, grand, and a little vain. When you dance to Imenja, you are praising her and asking for her blessings."

His students practiced the step across the studio. They ranged in age from adolescence to middle age and wore sarongs, bracelets, and beads. Several of the women wore anklets made of cowrie shells, which sounded like leaves rustling in the wind when they danced.

"Imenja is most feminine and beautiful of all the *orishas*," Meia Noite went on. "When you want love and beauty, beautiful man, beautiful woman to come into your life, you dance to Imenja and ask her to help you." Everyone laughed. The drums resumed and the dancers moved across the floor. Meia picked up a shaker and played with the drummers while he watched his students. One woman had problems with the step, and Meia went over to do the step with her. He held her hand until she got it right.

Delia felt her body rock to the rhythm of the drums. She stood in the doorway moving her hand, watching. She could almost hear a melody in the percussion, and then realized that Meia and some of the drummers were singing to Imenja. Everyone—the drummers, the dancers, the children playing their instruments, the older woman who could only lope through the steps but did so with an earthy grace—was united. All were caught in a web of movement, rhythm, and prayer that they had spun together. Delia longed to be a part of it. She stood in the doorway dancing with them. Meia spotted her and laughed.

"Little ballerina," he called to her. "Come dance with us." Delia started to explain why she couldn't, but then, like a sixth sense, she realized Madame Elanova had just walked by. Delia turned and saw her enter the costume room down the hall. Afraid she might be caught alone with Madame in the hall, she dashed back to the big studio where rehearsal for *Adagio Classique* had already resumed.

Quietly, Delia slipped into the circle surrounding Miss Dorain. She was lecturing the girls about their feet. She was angry.

"If I give one correction, I'm not going to repeat myself two or three times. You must point your feet. You must walk as if you were holding on to air. *DEL-I-CATE-LY!* Alicia, show them the costume."

At the back of the studio, Madame held the ivory costume to her body. The straps were thin, the bodice plain, and the long tulle skirt began at the hip and fell just above the ankles.

"Look!" commanded Miss Dorain. "The audience will be focusing on your *feet*!"

"You must point your feet!" reiterated

Madame. "You must valk lightly! I have not trained you to be farmers marching in boots!"

The girls accepted her words silently. Delia stood with her hands folded neatly in front of her, trying to look attentive.

"And you!" said Madame, pointing right at her. "You are shaming this school by sneaking in late to Miss Dorain's rehearsal. And vhat vere you doing instead? Learning dance of superstitious, illiterate people who know nothing about art. You are to be here, learning choreography of great Monsieur Prokov. Alvays on time! Alvays ready to learn! It is great honor for you, or are you too stupid to know this?"

Delia's heart seemed to freeze on the spot. At the same time her face felt as if it had caught fire. From the corner of her eye she saw a few of the girls stifle a laugh. The embarrassment made her feel sick, and she wished that the earth beneath her might collapse and swallow her.

At the end of rehearsal, Delia waited outside in the biting February afternoon for her father to pick her up. The gray trees scratched each other in the wind. It was nearly dark. In the foyer of the school Claire had struck up a conversation with the anorexics. Delia watched her through the glass door. She did not come outside to wait with her as she usually did.

Suddenly, Delia wanted nothing more than to be in the car with her father so that just this once, when he asked how rehearsal went, Delia would say something other than "fine." She wanted to tell him the whole story, about losing the part to Claire, Miss Dorain's abruptness, and the public shaming she had just received.

Her father pulled into the driveway and leaned across the passenger seat to open the door for Delia.

Ask me.

"Why weren't you waiting inside?" he asked. "It's too cold to be outside." He waited until Delia fastened her safety belt to drive away.

Ask me.

"Why didn't you wait inside with Claire?"

"I was okay."

It was dark now. Soon they would be home. Slowly the desire to tell her father what had happened stopped sweeping through her. It contracted, turning thin and sharp, and lodged between her ribs. Delia inhaled and exhaled deeply and felt the place where it hurt.

"Are you all right?" her father asked.

"I pulled a muscle," she said, pointing to her heart. Delia took another breath and felt the little stab of pain. She told her father part of the story. "I didn't get the part. Claire did. I'm just the understudy."

"Oh, honey," he said. "I'm sorry. I know how much you wanted it." They were home. "Don't worry. Just keep working hard and you'll get the part you want in the next performance." Delia didn't respond.

At home there was a phone message from Pearl.

"Little Moon, call me! Call me right now! I mean it!" Her voice was playful.

But Delia did not have the energy to call her back. The wound between her ribs had weakened her, and all she wanted to do was get in bed. She fell into bed and slept, dreamless and dark. It was as if she disappeared.

17

Wound

"You're lucky you caught me," said Pearl. "I was on my way to the stables."

"I thought I was going to wake you up," said Delia. "You never get up before noon on a weekend."

"Well, Little Moon, these days I'm up before dawn."

"You? I don't believe it. Why?"

"Hades," said Pearl, and she went on to outline the most recent development in her attempts to train the wild black horse. Finally, after days and weeks, he had let her slip on a bridle. "He's stopped tossing his head so

much, and he let me lead him around the cor-
ral. That's what I called to tell you."

"That's wonderful," said Delia. She felt it,
too, but mostly she was relieved her sister had
not asked her about Madame, the amulet, or
ballet. Delia described the weather and their
father's latest cycling outfit.

"It's lime green."

"Oh, stop," said Pearl.

"I'm serious. Keep me posted about Hades.
I've gotta get ready for rehearsal . . ."

"How's that going?"

"Just great," Delia lied.

At rehearsal Delia marked the steps in the
corner. She refrained from dancing full out
because she didn't want to draw attention to
herself. The thought of any sort of attention
from Madame or Miss Dorain, whether it be
praise or criticism, was unbearable.

At the end of rehearsal, Miss Dorain
received a round of thunderous applause. She
said her good-byes to the Elanova girls and

announced that she would not be returning until the dress rehearsal in early April. She reminded them of the great legacy of Russian training that Madame Elanova was passing down to them and told them to listen to everything she said. "She knows this ballet as well as I do."

"Oh, no, Christine." Madame laughed her most musical laugh, and Delia hated the artifice in it.

Days passed. Madame took over rehearsals for *Adagio Classique*. During these rehearsals, Madame only spoke to her twice. Once she praised her for marking the steps behind the others. Another time she told her she should be practicing the steps on pointe like everyone else.

"Vhat vould happen if someone else became sick and couldn't dance? You are very important person in the Elanova Ballet! I need you to be prepared!" It was a crumb of praise wrapped around another scolding. Delia knew she would never dance *Adagio Classique*. It was a patronizing remark, and the frustration she felt because she had no response made her want to cry.

Pointe class was much the same, and Delia came to dread it. For now, Delia was not a student of promise. She was an understudy, and Madame waved her to the back of the line in the last group. She looked bored or distracted when Delia bowed to her at the end of class. One day in the middle of barre, Madame delivered a long lecture about the dangers of gaining weight in the first two years after the onset of menstruation. Mr. Guest turned pink with embarrassment and began to organize an enormous pile of music.

"This is the time vhen your body decides vhat kind of woman you vill be—a dancer or a fat lady. If you let yourself get fat, even a little fat, your body vill never let go of it. Your body vill think it vants to become fat. That is vhy you must give up all fattening foods for these two years. At my ballet school in Russia, no girls between twelve and fifteen vere allowed to eat desserts. Sometimes, vhen ve vent on our outings to museum or botanical gardens, old ladies on the streetcars used to give us bits of chocolate. 'Poor little ballet rats,' they called us. I vas alvays very disciplined, so I alvays said no. Many girls did not say no and they became fat and had to leave. It is a sad story, but it is true. Many girls ruin their bodies at your age." Madame looked around the studio. Girls stood at the barre, attentive and still. "Cynthia, darling, finally you are looking good. You, Delia, I see more fat here, and here." Madame pointed to her stomach and hips. She singled out a few other girls. "All of you must be very careful. Already I see fat ladies vaiting to be born."

The remark hit Delia between the ribs. It entered the first wound like a blade and cut it fresh. *I won't leave class early*, she told herself. She turned deep within and found a small flame of strength. *I need you*, she told it. It took all the strength she had to dance the center combinations like everyone else. But the thought of putting her hand in Madame's and bowing at the end of class was too much. She left quietly before révérence. She changed quickly and waited outside for her father to pick her up.

The other girls began to shun her as if she were a leper. No one shared a joke or asked to borrow tape for a blister. No one chatted with her before class or in the changing room. Even Claire changed. She aligned herself with the others, for Delia had become an object of fear. Most of Madame's sylphs realized that what had happened to Delia could happen to any of them. Not associating with her, not recognizing her existence was the only way they knew to guard against a similar fate.

Occasionally, Delia let herself fantasize about becoming a different person. She thought about quitting ballet and changing schools. She would start her teenage years over by becoming a girl who played team sports, joined clubs, and went to dances and football games. What could it possibly be like, she wondered. What did it take to be popular at school, to have friends who called her on the phone, and went with her to the mall? She hadn't the foggiest idea. It couldn't be more difficult than what she was going through now.

In the end, the fantasy left her feeling empty. How could she possibly stop dancing? What would she do with everything that she had learned? She counted the things she knew on her fingers, rare things, beautiful things. She knew how to breathe through a phrase of movement so that her body was never still. She knew how to dance on top of a melody so that it felt like she was not a body moving to music, but the music itself. She knew how to speak in movement, how to send a prayer simply by opening her arms in port de bras. And she knew that if she quit dancing instead of rising to this terrible challenge Madame had thrust upon her, she would feel like a failure for the rest of her life.

She decided to get beyond these recent setbacks. She would go on a diet and lose as much weight as possible. Madame would forget she ever saw her dancing with the Brazilian class, and when the performance of *Adagio Classique* was over, Delia could start fresh. Madame would watch her, and, once again, she would be a sylph.

Delia willed the wound in her side to close. She imagined herself ethereal and serene, and she worked harder in class even though Madame no longer knew she existed.

18

Lies

For two weeks Delia lived on celery, carrots, hard-boiled eggs, nonfat yogurt, rice cakes, and diet soda. She kept her diet secret from her father by telling him she wanted to eat dinner in her room. Then she took the food he prepared for her, wrapped it up in newspaper, and threw it in the trash when he had left the kitchen.

Alone in her room she looked at herself in the mirror. Her ribs showed, and her knees and elbows were beginning to look big, but there was still a roundness to her tummy and hips. *I'm not skinny enough,* she thought in despair. Scared and frustrated that her weight loss was slowing down, she made her father take her to Theater Arts to buy her a pair of vinyl sweatpants.

"But these are what wrestlers wear when they're crash-dieting to reach their weight class! I hope you're not trying to lose weight!"

"I'm not, Dad," she lied. She had taken to wearing layers of shirts and leg warmers under her pants to hide her thinness from her father. "I've pulled a muscle in my hip joint and I need to keep it warm. These are the best things for that. One of the older girls told me. They all use them when they pull a muscle." It was another lie. None of the older girls was speaking to her these days, and only the anorexics wore the rubber sweatpants. They had begun to acknowledge her existence. They greeted her with slightly raised eyebrows when she wore the vinyl pants in pointe class.

She arrived early to class and gave herself a long, strenuous warm-up. She practiced her pirouettes over and over again in empty studios. When the blisters from her pointe shoes bled, she wound tape around them, pushed past the pain, and finished class.

At first she appreciated the hunger. She was airy and limber, and her bones felt light and flexible like the bones of a fish. By afternoon she felt spacey and cut off from everything around her. It was easy to walk the halls of Markham Middle School lapsed into her own world. Sometimes in ballet class, she even forgot the problems with Madame and danced for herself.

"You are looking very nice, my dear," Madame said to her at the barre one day. "Just a little bit more around the hips."

"Thank you, Madame," Delia whispered. Her heart leaped, and she danced with some of the vivacity she had when she was first told she was a sylph. She felt proud to go to bed hungry that night.

In the following weeks, however, Madame gave her no other scraps of praise. She focused on the girls in *Adagio Classique*, reminding them to practice this or that segment of choreography.

"No!" she said to a member of the corps. "This is same mistake you make in *Adagio Classique*. Your feet in entrechat are sloppy and veak. You are only girl in line vith this problem. Do it again and point your feet!" Every time Madame mentioned the ballet or the girls talked about it in the dressing room, Delia felt more and more alone. She was substandard and insufficient, and the only way she knew how to improve was to work harder and stay hungry.

But the hunger no longer helped her dance. She began to feel so light-headed that there were times when she thought she might faint. At the barre, during développés and rond de jambe en l'air, two steps that need the perfect combination of flexibility and strength, she saw stars.

She began to feel even weaker. No longer could she complete her homework during lunch at school or at the break between ballet class and rehearsal. She had lost her ability to do two things at once, and she even had trouble doing her homework on the days when there was no rehearsal. There were days when even a pen felt heavy in her hand, and at night she often fell asleep at her desk trying to complete her assignments.

"What's going on?" whispered Mr. McGrath as he handed a failed test to Delia. It was the third failing grade she had received on a history test this term. "Is something wrong?"

Delia looked at the paper. It was riddled with red marks. A big F floated at the top of the page.

"I . . ." began Delia, unsure of what she was going to say. Should she tell him about being cut from *Adagio Classique*? About Madame Elanova? "I think I have mono," she lied.

"Have you gone to the doctor?" he asked.

"Not yet."

"Well, get yourself to a doctor! You look terrible—pale and tired and skinny! Mononucleosis can be very serious! Have you had a blood test?"

"I'm seeing the doctor today. After school," Delia lied. She knew mono was going around Markham Middle School. Her lab partner in science had been out with it for weeks.

"Good!" said Mr. McGrath. "You've got to take care of yourself, little dancer." *If he only knew.* She was no longer a sylph. She was a liar. Delia turned away from him and put the test in a folder.

Later Delia was relieved when Claire apologized for not being able to eat lunch with her as usual. She felt too tired to put forth the effort to keep up a sunny facade. They rendezvoused at their table, but Claire only stayed long enough to wolf down a small tin of tuna.

"I have a test to make up," she said cheerily. She flipped her dark, slippery ponytail over her shoulder. She had taken to constantly wearing a short leg warmer over her left ankle, even at school. Her tendinitis was acting up, she explained. She marched pluckily out of the cafeteria, feet turned out, ponytail swishing from side to side. Delia ate her rice cakes alone. There seemed to be a draft in the building, and she wrapped her sweater tighter around herself.

"I'm sick," she told her father when she got home. The walk from the bus stop had worn her out. Whether she was truly sick or not, Delia didn't know, but she couldn't face class and rehearsal. "I can't go to ballet." She leaned against the wall.

"Let me feel your forehead," said Mr. Ferri. "I think you have a fever." He sent her to bed, took her temperature, and brought her some tea. Her temperature was normal, so he tried to convince her to eat. "What can I fix you?" he asked.

"Nothing. I'm nauseous," Delia lied. "I just need to rest."

When her father left, Delia cried. Anything she allowed herself to think of intensified her tears. She worried about Mr. McGrath thinking he was wrong to ever have a high opinion of her. She worried about Madame criticizing her again in front of the class. She worried about what the sylphs would think of her if they knew she was faking an illness to get out of rehearsal. Maybe what Pearl said was true—maybe her commitment to ballet and Madame just replaced the sadness she felt because she didn't have a mother. Maybe she was never meant to be a dancer at all. What she wanted most was to wake up as a different person, someone who never disappointed Madame or her father or her teachers. She could never tell her father how Madame had been treating her lately. It was better to lie. *But I'm so lonely*, she thought.

19

Delirium

The next day, home from school, Delia lay on her bed staring at the ceiling, too weak to read or watch TV. She napped and dreamed of falling and running, of being unable to open a door, or say her name.

She went to the doctor and he took her temperature and some blood samples. He checked her ears and her eyes and listened to her heart. She was anemic and weak, too thin and overtired, but other than that, he did not find anything seriously wrong with her. She had no fever, her glands were not swollen, so he doubted she had mono.

"What I am most concerned about," he told Delia and her father in his office, "is her weight loss." He studied her chart silently while Delia glanced at the photographs on his desk. They must be of his family, she thought. "Right now, she weighs eleven pounds less than she did at her twelve-year checkup. Have you been dieting, Delia?"

"No," she lied. "I'm so tired from dancing that sometimes I can't eat."

"And how many hours a week have you been dancing?"

"Well, not counting rehearsals, I'd say about ten hours a week."

"Why not count rehearsals?"

"Because you don't really dance full out in a rehearsal. There's a lot of stopping and starting."

"Go ahead and count the rehearsals. How many hours would it be then?"

"I'd say between fifteen and eighteen hours a week."

The doctor scribbled some more notes into her file and shook his head. "Ah, well, you see this is too much," he said. He looked Delia in the eyes and spoke in a stern voice. "Your body is still growing. It needs lots of rest and lots of healthy food. You're denying it both of these things, and you could become very, very sick. You might develop anorexia nervosa. Have you heard of this disease before? No? Well, it is very serious indeed. Sometimes girls your age even have to be hospitalized because of it." He went on to prescribe three weeks of bed rest and a healthy diet. "Plenty of fruits and vegetables, fish and meat, potatoes, et cetera. Make an appointment with the nutritionist on the way out. No school for three weeks, and no ballet for a month. Have her teachers send work home."

Mr. Ferri, worried and frightened, shook his hand and thanked him. He ushered Delia into the car and fastened her safety belt as if she were a child. Delia felt the caring and love in the gesture, but she felt too blurred and faded to cry.

Later in the afternoon, Mr. Ferri returned from Markham Middle School. He had met with the principal to explain Delia's absence and to get some homework for her. A pile of books and folders waited for her on the breakfast table.

"I was surprised when he told me that you were failing three out of five classes! He said he hoped you would be able to keep up with your classes and raise your grades at the same time, but that we should probably consider summer school. Delia, why didn't you tell me you were having problems at school?"

Delia stared at the pile of papers and books. Just the sight of them made her feel exhausted. "I didn't know I was failing any classes," she lied.

"Your history teacher is being very nice about it. He wrote me this note." Delia read it silently.

*I am saddened by Delia's poor performance
in my class. She used to be my top student.
I am confident she will regain her high
standing once she fully recovers from her
recent bout of mononucleosis.*

"Why does he think you have mono?" her
father asked.

"He must have me mixed up with someone else. It's going around the school,"
offered Delia. She felt angry at herself for
making her father worry. That was Pearl's
job, not hers.

*I am happy to help her in any way I can.
When she is feeling better, I'd like her to
see me about an extra credit project that
will help raise her grade to a passing
one. I've put some thought into this, and
I think I have a topic that Delia will
enjoy learning about.*

"You should take him up on his offer," said Mr. Ferri.

"I will," said Delia.

Mr. Ferri slapped the table. "Excellent!" he said. "We'll get you back on track in no time!"

What had she become, Delia wondered as she drifted back through the hall to her room. She was no longer strong and disciplined, and she was not a good dancer nor a good student. She began to wonder if someone really had cursed her the way Pearl had described. Was it Claire because she wanted the part so badly? Was it because she had embarrassed Madame in front of Miss Dorain? All she knew was that she felt weak and ashamed, unable to figure out why all of this had happened.

The night before the performance of *Adagio Classique*, Delia woke suddenly. Her heart was beating fast, and she felt as if she were being chased, but she had no memory of the nightmare. Her hair and brow were damp with perspiration. She had a strong feeling that something mean was watching her from the corner of her room. She pulled out Pearl's amulet from her dresser and put it around her neck. *Pearl. Pearl.* She tried conjuring her sister. She wanted some of her sister's fierceness. *I need you.* She curled up in bed, holding the amulet against herself, and fell asleep.

20

Performance

It was the night of the performance of *Adagio Classique*, and Delia was torn between wanting to go and wanting to stay home. She wanted to see the Elanova dancers in this important work, and she especially wanted to see how Cynthia fared. She even had a rose to give to Claire after the performance, but she was still uneasy. She did not want to discuss her illness with anyone or explain why she stopped attending rehearsals. And, after staying home in bed for so long, she had gained back most of the weight she had lost, and the thought of seeing Madame or Miss Dorain made her cringe. She wished Pearl was with her. She took another look at herself in the mirror, making sure the amulet she wore under her dress was out of sight. Fortunately, her father was coming with her. She would let him explain the mysteries and intricacies of her illness to anyone who asked.

The theater was bustling with excitement. Madame Elanova had donned her performance uniform—black dress, silk scarf tied at the neck, slightly too much makeup. She held court in the lobby, introducing Miss Dorain to a few carefully chosen parents, and gesturing regally. Miss Dorain looked like an aged tropical bird. She was swathed in a red and purple chiffon dress, her too-skinny arms poking out from the filmy fabric like sticks. Her hair was pulled into a messy bun. Fathers and siblings roamed the lobby. The familiar flock of stage mothers was busy manning a booth of handicrafts designed to raise a few dollars for the fledgling company. Allegra arrived on crutches with a small entourage of friends and admirers.

The little girl from Pointes One, daughter of the family Allegra was living with, solemnly carried the program of the injured princess.

Claire's parents waved energetically at Delia and Mr. Ferri as they walked down the aisle of the theater. They invited them to sit in the two seats next to them. They were touched that Delia had brought Claire a rose and expressed concern over her illness. Somehow they, too, had heard that she was suffering from mononucleosis. Delia let the remarks pass without comment. Her father said he appreciated their concern, but gave no details about the nature of Delia's illness. Delia felt pleasantly remote and participated minimally in the necessary social niceties. She had successfully avoided Madame and Miss Dorain. She felt much better than she thought she was going to. She was almost enjoying herself. And then, the music to *Adagio Classique* began.

For the first few bars of music the curtain remained closed, then it rose on the tableau of the entire corps in the pose Delia had been praised for. They stood with their feet parallel, right hand raised, eyes looking beyond the line of the hand, what was it Miss Dorain said, to heaven? To God? The image caught Delia in the throat, and if she had been less self-conscious, she would have cried out. She saw Claire standing in her place, and the desire to be dancing to the music was physically painful.

The company danced with security, if not expression. The anorexics whirled confidently, and Cynthia was generous and spirited in the lift of her torso and expanse of her arms. The older sylphs were practiced and refined, and the destined one danced the leading role with a regal confidence. Madame was correct—the choreography suited her. It came to her as essentially and easily as air. If he were alive watching from the wings, surely the great Prokov would have said something like, "That girl . . . that girl . . . Who is that girl? I want her in my company."

The audience applauded wildly. Grandparents wiped away tears. Little sisters were mesmerized. Brothers woofed and arfed. Fathers and mothers dried damp eyes. Delia wanted to leave as soon as possible.

"Here," Delia said to Claire's mother once the curtain dropped after the final curtain calls. "Would you give this to Claire for me?" Delia handed Claire's mother the rose.

"Aren't you going to the party at Madame's apartment after the performance?" she asked. "I'm sure Claire and the other girls would love to see you. Allegra is going. It's for the understudies as well."

"Oh, no. I'm not up to it. I still don't feel very good."

Mr. Ferri took his daughter's cue swiftly. "Yes," he chimed in. "This has been a late night for Delia. She needs to go home."

On the drive home, Delia shunned her father's entreaties to talk. She couldn't possibly tell him what she was feeling. She didn't know herself.

"I'm too tired to have a conversation," she said, and turned her head to look out the window. She pulled the amulet out from under her dress and pinched it until she felt the lump of beeswax and remembered Pearl's wish for her. Strength. It seemed so far away, as far away as the dancers on the stage.

The next day, a letter from Pearl arrived. Her father brought it in with her lunch on a tray.

Dearest Little Moon,

We keep missing each other and haven't really talked since Christmas vacation. I guess it's as much my fault as yours—you're as caught up with your dancing as I am with my witchcraft. But there are things I want to share with you, so I'm writing this letter. Hopefully it will come out the way I want it to . . .

I've been thinking about what you said on Christmas about the pictures I gave you and Dad, and I think you're right. It was selfish. I was trying to get you and Dad to feel something for Mom, and it was wrong of me. You see, for so long I've thought that Dad has either forgotten her or erased her from his memory. It made me feel like he was doing the same thing to me, because Mom is part of me. I have half her genes and half her blood, and if Dad was trying to forget her, he was trying to forget me. I was so angry with him, and I wanted to force him to remember her. So I gave him back the picture I stole. But it didn't work the way I wanted. And when I thought about it later, I realized maybe the reason that he never talks about her isn't because he's forgotten her. It's because he can't forget her. Maybe he's just too sad to ever really talk about her, and that's why he's turned into such a maniac about cycling, and keeps working so much at the bakeries even though he hired a manager to run them . . . And I wanted to tell you that I was sorry for trying to force you to feel something for Mom. If you don't, you don't—it's not up to me to make you feel one thing or the other about her.

I suppose you'll want to know how I came to all of these realizations, and if I had to come up with an answer I would say it's because of Hades, my horse at school. He's so wild. He still won't let me ride him. For the longest time he wouldn't even take a sugar cube from me or let me brush his mane. I kept trying to win his trust, speaking in a lower voice one day, bringing him an apple another day, thinking up different spells. But you know what? Nothing I did changed him. I had to wait until he changed. In the meantime, I had to slow down and quit trying so hard to figure him out. He still doesn't fully trust me, but just before I came home he let me put on his saddle. Maybe that's as far as we'll ever get.

So, what I'm trying to say, Little Moon, is that I know now that I can't change the way you or Dad feel about Mom or anything else. I know that now, and even though I'm still sad and lonely because it seems like I'm the only one who wants any kind of connection with Mom anymore, I don't feel so angry. I'm even getting to like school again. The Highton School really isn't such a bad place.

Remember that I love you, Little Moon. If you look inside the envelope, you'll find a tiny little owl feather. I combed it out of Hades's mane. The owl is the special bird for Athena, goddess of wisdom and clarity, you know. Keep it close.

Love and kisses,
Pearl

Delia looked in the corners of the envelope and found a downy feather no bigger than the nail of her thumb. She held it in her palm, blew it into the air, and caught it. Pearl's words circled in her mind. Sentences broke apart and rejoined, images of her mother and Madame, her father and Pearl floated in her mind and settled. Pearl's letter set off a dozen questions that split and fractured into a dozen more. Had her father tried to ignore Pearl because she looked so much like her mother? Was Pearl right that you can't change other people? Could she ever make Madame see her the way she did the day she called her a sylph? All she knew was that, in spite of everything, she still wanted to dance. And the only way she could do so was to rest and get stronger so that she could return to ballet with all that she needed to regain Madame's attention.

21

Vision

In the last days of Delia's bed rest, cherry trees bloomed all over Washington. They bloomed in gardens and parks, around monuments, townhouses, and in the yard of the house where Delia lived. Tight green buds grew swollen and exploded into clusters of pink blossoms. Delia watched them and felt strong and self-contained, ready to return to the world outside her bedroom.

"It was mono," said Delia. It was her first day back at Markham Middle School after her three weeks of bed rest. She and Claire were catching up in the hall between classes.

"That's what I heard!" commiserated Claire. "How awful for you! You missed all those fabulous rehearsals with Miss Dorain. I swear to you she really does channel Andrew Prokov. She called out to him in the middle of dress rehearsal and begged him to help us with that piqué arabesque section."

"I believe it," said Delia. "I feel lucky I had the time with her that I did. Oh, well . . . those are the breaks."

"Are you coming to class today?" asked Claire.

"Not today, but soon. I'm not strong enough yet. I'll probably start next week."

"I'm so glad!" said Claire. "I've missed you so much!"

Sure, thought Delia. She felt guarded and suspicious around Claire. She remembered how quickly she dropped her and started hanging out with the anorexics, of all people, once Madame started picking on her. She was no friend.

The bell rang, and the girls darted off in separate directions.

"See you tomorrow," Claire sang cheerfully.

"Okay!" answered Delia.

Lockers slammed and chattering students bounced down the hall. Delia took it all in and walked deliberately down the hall. She wasn't a bit lost in thoughts of music or ballet. She was fully there, feeling the floor beneath her feet and the little rushes of air as students darted around her. She copied notes from the board and wrote the details of her homework assignments in her planner. Markham Middle School felt familiar and safe, and she wasn't at all sad to be back.

Unfortunately, Delia lost much of this new strength once she returned to ballet class. It disappeared like a scarf in the wind as soon as she walked through the door of the Elanova School. She felt like the unwanted stepsister, as if the entire circle of sylphs had sung "tick-tock, the game is locked" while she was away. Madame did not welcome her back. She ignored her in class, except for saying, "Excellent, Delia!" when she completed three perfect pirouettes. Claire pretended to be in a great hurry at all times, and the anorexics looked right through her. Even the expressionless Mr. Guest seemed to treat her as if she were nothing but a piece of dust. He coughed every time she walked by.

Once again Delia felt threatened and alone. She worried Madame might start harping on her about her weight. So, she hung at the back of the studio, and chose a place at the barre where Madame rarely looked. She danced in the back line of the last group, and when she bowed to Madame at the end of class, she dropped her gaze so their eyes never met.

Sometimes at night when she could not sleep, Delia racked her brain, trying to figure out why she had fallen from Madame's graces. Surely it was not just because she watched a few moments of Brazilian class. She recalled Madame's early comment about her legs and feet being like Pavlova's. She remembered how Christine Dorain had said aloud in front of the entire cast that only she had the correct feeling in the opening pose of *Adagio Classique*. Had she embarrassed Madame in front of Christine Dorain by being inattentive? Did Madame think she had made a great mistake when she had found so much promise in her only a few months ago and was this her way of telling her? Was it just like Claire had once said, that Madame always had to pick on someone in rehearsals? And was her time for abuse now over and would Madame move on to someone else? Delia thought of Cynthia and all the humiliations she had endured. The thought of years like the month she had just experienced was unbearable. Is this what it took to become a professional ballet dancer?

At home she was busy making up the work she missed and writing the extra credit report Mr. McGrath had assigned so she could pass American history. The topic was the ghost dance religion of the Plains Indians, and he had lent her some of his own books.

Finally, one day, she decided to approach Madame and ask her why she had treated her so cruelly. She would ask her after pointe class on Wednesday afternoon. To give herself strength, she pinned Pearl's amulet to the inside of her leotard. After class, she followed Madame to the office and knocked on the door. Madame was looking through some photographs. She waved her in.

"Delia! How are you? How nice it is to see you in class again."

"Thank you, Madame. I'm glad to be back," she lied. "But I have to ask you something."

"And vhat is that?"

"I want to know what I did wrong. I want to know if you were angry at me because I had gained weight or if there was something else. . . . I want to know why you gave the role in *Adagio Classique* to Claire, and why you embarrassed me in front of everyone, and then ignored me."

"Delia," she said coolly, "you ask so many questions. Some do not have answers . . . I vas never angry vith you. I never vanted to humiliate you. Maybe I hurt your feelings, but you gained veight. I had to tell you. You vill never be a dancer if you do not stay thin."

"But you made me feel like I couldn't dance, that I was nothing, that I wasn't fit to be here."

"I didn't mean to make you feel this, but, Delia, I must be honest vith you. You have many gifts for a ballet dancer, but all in all, I do not think you have the temperament to dance. You are too sensitive and shy. You do not know how to fight for a part. You gave up too easily. There are many girls vith pretty feet and legs. There are many girls who have talent. In the end, such things do not mean very much. Yes, a ballerina must have these things, but she must have something more. A dancer must be resilient and strong. She must never let vhat anyone says or does stop her, no matter how much it hurts her feelings."

"But why did you say such nice things to me when I first came to your school?"

"Because you do have talent, but not so very much. You are not extraordinary. For you to succeed, you must vork very hard. You must devote your entire self to ballet, and you can never let a mean look from another student or a criticism from a teacher stop you. Perhaps, at twenty, you vill be in the corps de ballet of a nice company, but I doubt you vill ever be a soloist. You vill never be a principal in a great company. Aftervards, vhen you are too old or injured to dance, you vill teach. Is this the life you vant? You are lucky you are so young. You have a few more years to answer this question. And now, I must get back to vork. You think about vhat I have said, and you make your decision. Maybe you do not vant to study ballet any longer. Maybe this is your last season at the Elanova School."

Delia walked out to the street. Cars and buses drove by. People entered and left offices and stores, houses and apartments on Wisconsin Avenue. They were going out to dinner, returning home from work, running errands, and meeting friends without music or choreography in their heads. It was incomprehensible to Delia. She watched them and cried because when she quit dancing, she would become like them.

Madame had given her a choice—either to work harder and feel less, or quit. *I'll quit,*

Delia decided, *but not before the session ends.* She would not give Madame the victory of making her stop dancing so shortly after their talk. And then she would be one of the people on the street.

Delia put away all her love for dancing and music. She closed her eyes and saw them as two white spirits drawn to an open box like a genie to its lamp, insubstantial as smoke. The box closed and locked, and she threw a pretend key out her bedroom window and saw it vanish into a black sky. *There. You're gone now.*

In the days to follow, Delia learned how to ignore her heart when she heard a favorite piece of music in class. It wasn't that hard. It was like not eating when you were hungry or dancing on pointe when you had blisters.

Slowly but surely, Madame lost her power over Delia. She stopped working so hard in class. She couldn't care less when she fell out of pirouettes or messed up a combination. She didn't bother to bow to her after class. Instead, she walked brazenly out of the studio and coughed back at Mr. Guest. She was beginning to understand something about Pearl and she liked it. She couldn't wait until the school year was over and they would be together at home.

Letters from Pearl were less frequent. "I'm sorry I'm not writing more often," she wrote in one.

I'm actually studying. Between riding Hades (yes, I'm riding him now) and hitting the books, I don't have any time on my hands. But I've been thinking about things, and I've come up with a plan. I want to be a horse trainer. The one here says I have the touch, and that no one else has ever gotten as far with Hades as I have. And I've loved every bit of it, even

the weeks when he'd hardly let me near
him. I get to use everything I ever learned
from witchcraft with him, and the whole
process feels so mythic and empowering
that I've decided that it's how I want to
spend my life . . .

Pearl with a passion and a goal . . . Delia could scarcely believe it. She read the letter again before putting it away. She supposed she felt happy for her, but it made her ache for ballet, because she knew she might not ever want something that badly again.

"Look at this!" her father said gleefully one afternoon. He slapped a letter in Delia's lap. It was Pearl's midterm report. She was earning As in all of her classes. "There's only three weeks left in the term and she's on her way to straight As. Isn't that great?"

"Wow!" said Delia. "What's going on with her?"

"I found the right school for her! That's what happened! She's bound to get into college with grades like this!"

"I don't think she wants to go to college, Dad. I think she wants to . . ." But she stopped herself. It was up to Pearl to tell her father, not her.

"She's going to college. She doesn't have a choice in the matter. And neither do you, by the way."

It was pointless to argue, so Delia nodded and left the room.

In the last weeks of school, Delia buried herself in schoolwork. Her report on the ghost dance religion took on epic proportions. She read about the white man's invasion and how the Plains Indians were moved onto reservations. She read about poverty, disease, and starvation, and how in the darkest time, when it was clear to the Indians that their way of life was gone forever, a prophet came. His name was Wovoka, and he had talked with the Great Spirit. One day, he taught, the white man would disappear. Disease and suffering would be over, and all their dead ancestors, family, and friends would return from the spirit world. The buffalo would come back, and all Indians would be united in peace. Once again, the Indians would be powerful and free. To make themselves worthy of this change, Indians should dance the holy dance he had come to teach them.

Delia studied the drawings and diagrams of the dance in Mr. McGrath's book. Two circles of dancers, one inside the other, moved in opposite directions. They held hands, took three steps forward, reached down to the earth then up to the sky. The dancers repeated these movements over and over again, sometimes for as long as four days, singing the songs of the ghost dance.

Mother, come home; Mother, come home.
Your little child goes about always crying,
Your little child goes about always crying.
Mother, come home; Mother, come home.

Every now and then, a dancer broke from the circle, staggered into the middle of the ring, and fell in a trance. When he woke, he described his vision of the spirit world and how he was reunited with a dead wife, child, parent, or friend.

Delia wondered what it felt like to perform the dance. It was like a child's dance, and she couldn't imagine that it could make someone dream or go into a trance. She memorized the steps. It was so easy, simpler than the easiest combination in a beginning ballet class.

It was dark and cold outside, but Delia grew warm as she danced near the ring of stones Pearl had built years ago. Over and over she practiced the steps. She reached to the earth and thought of Pearl and how much she missed her. She reached to the sky and thought of ballet and how music spoke to her. She thought of her mother in the spirit world and tried to hear her voice. She could not. She became dizzy and fell, scraping her shin on one of the stones. The pain brought tears to her eyes, and she curled into a ball, holding herself on the ground and choking with sobs that came from deep inside but made no sound.

22

Spirit

Finally, the school year ended, and with it the spring session at the Elanova School. Delia made up all of her missing work, passed her classes, and even got an A in history. She told her father not to sign her up for summer classes at the Elanova School. She had quit ballet. When he asked her why, Delia said simply, "I'm sick of it."

One Saturday, she took the bus to the Elanova School at a time when she was sure neither Madame or any of the sylphs would be around. She needed to clean out her locker, where she had stuffed a favorite sweater. She wore a T-shirt and jeans, and her loose hair fell about her face. She could have been any teenage girl wandering in from the street.

The foyer was empty and the main studio was dark. Miss Dairy, loyal slave that she was, was bent over some paperwork at her desk. She didn't hear the door open. Delia skipped downstairs to the dressing room, grateful to find it empty as well. She whirled through the numbers of her combination, tied the old sweater around her waist, and dumped the padlock into her purse. It took less than a minute.

So intent was she on her mission that she did not hear the drums from the Brazilian class when she left the dressing room. It startled her when she heard them echoing loudly in the hall, and she decided to stop by the small studio and watch Meia's class.

Meia Noite and his students were dancing to a seductive rhythm set by a massive drum called a surdo. It sounded like an enormous heartbeat, and the dancers moved with it, shaking their hips and beckoning to the sky and the earth. One woman started laughing, and Meia laughed with her. As he raised his head, he caught Delia's eye and walked over to her.

"Why you never take my class? I can tell you want to learn Brazilian dance." His voice lilted in a velvety growl. He grinned at her mischievously. "Or maybe you are just a snobby ballet dancer?"

"I'm not a snobby ballet dancer," Delia answered. "I'm not any type of dancer. I quit."

Meia Noite scowled. He looked like an angry king. "Who told you such a thing is possible? A dancer cannot quit dancing."

His response was confusing. *But I'm not a dancer,* she wanted to say, but couldn't. She lifted a hand as if she were about to speak, then dropped it.

Meia Noite looked at her intently. He went on. "I see something in your eyes, something I have seen in other girls at this school. It is sadness," said Meia Noite. "I know now what has happened to you. That old woman has filled your head with lies. She has told you lies about yourself and lies about dance. The old woman has some wisdom, but she knows nothing about the spirit. Mostly, she is cruel." In the studio the drummers and dancers continued. Layers of rhythm echoed in the hall.

Delia could no longer meet Meia Noite's gaze. She was embarrassed by his insight, and all the love that she had for dance, the love that she had tried to work out of her and ignore, rose up inside her. It hurt to breathe, and when she managed to gulp some air, she began to cry.

"Look what that old woman has done to you," Meia whispered. "How can you let her turn you into a ghost?"

23

Ochumare

Mr. Ferri looked at his two girls. They wore leotards and sarongs, necklaces and bracelets of shells, wood, and bone. Delia looked like a temple dancer from a tropical island, so comfortable was she in the fall of the cloth and the music of her jewelry. For the first time in years Pearl's hair was its natural color—blond. She had worked it into dozens of tiny braids. Each one ended in a bead. Her face was clean, her skin glowing. She carried a small drum. She had been taking private lessons from Meia Noite ever since Delia had introduced her to him. *What strong spirits my daughters are*, he thought. *How bright and fierce they are.*

It was a Washington Saturday in August, lazy, expansive, and tropical. The river was friendly and slow, the trees drenched with green. Bees and butterflies gorged themselves on pollen, and enormous white clouds hung still in the sky. Pearl sped down Wisconsin Avenue to the Elanova School for Meia Noite's class.

The drummers had already begun playing, and Pearl took her place among them. Meia was embracing his students, saying hello to a young mother and kissing her child. The old woman with gray hair was there, as were college students and children, teenagers and adults who came from all over the city for his class.

"Little Moon," he said, hugging her. "Today we dance special dance to my *orisha*, Ochumare. You're gonna love it."

Meia took a drum and beat out a series of phrases for each section of drummers to follow.

The sound was multilayered and thick, with the surdo setting a strong, distinct rhythm under the other drums. The big drum sounded like soft thunder. It echoed in Delia's chest and massaged her heart.

Meia danced with his back to the class to demonstrate. He moved from side to side in crossing steps, his body rocking softly, his shoulders rolling back. His palms were open and welcoming.

The steps were simple, but they were difficult for Delia. She could not dance on the ground the way Meia Noite did. Her feet wanted to rise on half pointe, and her knees wanted to straighten. Ballet had trained her to pull out of the floor, as if she lived in the air instead of on the earth. She gave up rolling her shoulders and tried simply to step with her feet on the floor and her knees bent.

After a few minutes, Meia Noite stopped the drummers and explained the dance to his students.

"This is dance to Ochumare, orisha of creation and rebirth. In Brazil, we see him as a serpent, you see, because a serpent sheds his skin. A serpent is born many times in one life. This is a good lesson for us. When we move our head and body like this, we are asking Ochumare to take away our old life and bring us a new one. Come, let's try again."

Meia split the class into groups and had one line of dancers then another perform the steps across the floor. He danced with each group and took aside those who were having problems, teaching them by holding their hand. Slowly, Delia began to relax into the dance. The repetition of the drums and steps made Delia feel light-headed, and when she passed Pearl she stopped to say, "I think I'm going to start trancing."

"Yeah, well don't," said Pearl. "Meia's the only one who can get you out and he's gotta teach class." She moved her hips to the beat and shook her braids so they fell behind her shoulders. *She's getting good*, thought Delia. *She didn't miss a beat.*

Again and again Delia danced across the studio. She opened her hands to Ochumare, thanking him for this new life she had entered. Meia Noite watched her and said, "Yes, Little Moon. You know what it is to be reborn."

Delia smiled back at him and laughed. How big the world is, she thought, drums and sunlight in every cell of her body. How many dances there are to learn.

Also by Tracey Porter

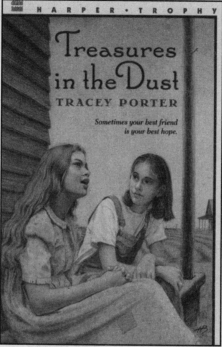

Pb 0-06-440770-5

Annie May Weightman and Violet Cobble are best friends living in Oklahoma during the Great Depression. While Annie is happiest on the ground, sifting the earth for traces of the past, Violet longs to escape the dusty land surrounding them. Their story is one of friendship and courage— treasures shining through in the face of hardship.

www.harperchildrens.com　　HarperTrophy®　　Joanna Cotler Books
An Imprint of HarperCollinsPublishers